PROLOGUE

his story, Gentle Reader, is one of magic and adventure, and is quite filled to bursting with a great many long-ago and legendary creatures. Indeed, there are so many that, to keep you from confusing the whatnots with the what-have-yous, we have included such notes as we could. Professor Algernon Aisling's journal of the voyage was helpful, and Miss Cassandra Aisling's later writings, too, were very useful. We also consulted, as frequently as patience allowed, the Oldest Professor and the renowned Book of Answers (about these you will hear *much* more later) as well.

Now if you don't like a story with magic and adventure and extraordinary creatures, well then! There's nothing to do but close your eyes this instant and go right to sleep. Unless, of course, you'd rather clean out your closet or write one thousand times, "I prefer to be terribly, terribly, *terribly* sensible."

But, Gentle Reader, if a magical journey aboard a magical ship is to your liking, come along; there isn't a moment to lose. There is magic afoot, and the Aisling family is about to meet it head on.

—THE GENTLEMEN OF THE COLLEGE
OF MAGICAL KNOWLEDGE

One evening late in April 1850, the Aisling family's world got turned upside down. Not just a little bit tilted, mind you, but wholly, truly and topsy-turvily tangled and tumbled into something that sensible folk wouldn't believe for a second.

Cassandra Aisling, who was nine years and eleven months old (which made her very, very close to ten), didn't care a jot what sensible people thought. Cassandra liked strange, mysterious and magical things, none of which you were likely to find by being sensible.

Cassandra's father, Professor Algernon Aisling, taught at a university, lecturing on mythology and ancient legends. Mythology and legends, as you may have heard, are absolutely full of strange, mysterious and magical things. So this made Professor Aisling a quite perfect father for Cassandra. There were people who said that the professor wasn't quite sensible, but Cassandra didn't care a jot about that, either. She liked his stories and that

Does progress mean that we must discard our ancient myths? If we forget our legends, I fear that we shall close an important door to the imagination. If only I could go exploring! Perhaps I would see the marvels that inspired the creators of our legends.

Nereids, oreids and dryads... nixies and pixies...forests full of faeries...stories for everyone who wants to dream.

There is magic and wonder out there.

What is out there in the other direction?

Medusa the Gorgon, from a Greek shield design. What could have inspired such a monstrous legend?

was that. But in recent months, there had been few stories. Not quite a year past, Mrs. Lily Aisling had been taken from them by a fever, and they all still missed her greatly. Of late, however, Cassandra had seen that her father's brow was even more furrowed in the evening when he returned home. Cassandra knew that something at the university troubled him.

Cassandra's sister, Miranda, hadn't been much company, either. Perhaps it was losing her mother, or turning sixteen (which is likely to make anybody think she should be sensible just in case someone is watching), but Miranda had suddenly decided to be all the way grown-up at once. Anyone who has ever tried this can tell you that it is a great deal of work. Cassandra thought it very dull.

Wouldn't it be wonderful to just sail away and find the magic?

But time passes, and the Aislings had once again begun to go walking along the River Thames as they had always done. On that evening in April, Miranda and Cassandra got out their bonnets as usual, and Cassandra called upstairs to their father very day a quite horrid little man by the name of Bilgewallow had told the professor that mythology was silly and that the university would soon be done with such nonsense. You can imagine how that made Professor Aisling feel. What would the

Miranda Aisling

Named after Shakespeare's heroine in "The Tempest." She hadn't an idea of how necessary she was to the adventure.

Professor Algernon Aisling

Lectured on mythology. Had great faith in the power of imagination. Believed in the wisdom of legends.

Cassandra Aisling

Named after the Greek prophetess of Troy who, cursed by the gods, could foretell the future, though no one believed her.

to come down. She knew he was at his desk, writing worrisome thoughts in his journal.

Cassandra didn't mention this to her elder sister. When you are nine years and eleven months old, a great many people are likely to think that you still belong in the cradle (especially older sisters). And, it so happens, young ladies named Cassandra have been having a difficult time being listened to for ages.

What Cassandra didn't know was that on that world be like without all the old magical stories?

When he at last left his desk, Cassandra pulled at his sleeve. "Daddy, we've been waiting *hours*. Please let's hurry. I want to see the first star come out." Her father tweaked a lock of her hair.

"Lucky thing we didn't name you Patience," he said. She giggled and swung the door wide, and then jumped down the front steps two at a time. Miranda gave her father a shy smile and followed her younger sister.

As they walked toward London's river, the professor asked himself, "Are the old stories no longer of use?" and he answered himself immediately. "Of course they are!" he said aloud, which made Miranda glance at him and wish he'd be sensible and not talk to himself. "Imagination is where science begins!" the professor explained, thumping his stick. "Not with charts and tools and measurements. First the idea, *then* the experiment!" And he thumped his stick down again.

"Father," whispered Miranda, "please stop talking to yourself. People will look at us."

"Eh? What?" asked her father, looking around just in time to miss stepping in a puddle. Then he sighed. "I wish I'd thought to say all that to Bilgewallow this morning."

"You wish you had said what, Daddy?" asked Cassandra, slipping her hand into his.

"That one's imagination is where science starts, because you have to have the idea first, and that the old myths are one of the ways to keep your imagination working."

Cassandra didn't quite know what he was talking about, but she did like the myths because they

Mr. Bilgewallow, a member of the university, is given to snorting and harrumphing. "Anything that can't be weighed or measured or dissected," said he, "is just nonsense!"

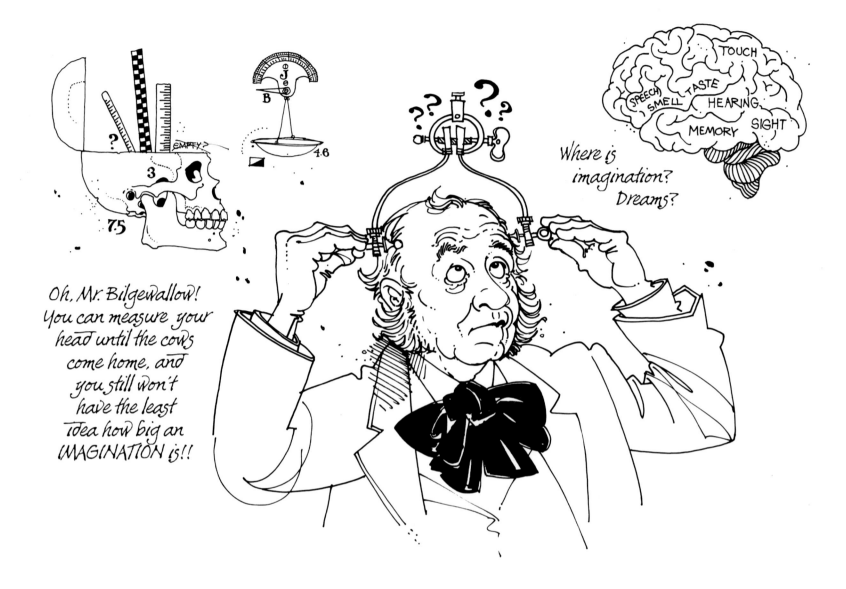

Oh, Mr. Bilgewallow! You can measure your head until the cows come home, and you still won't have the least idea how big an IMAGINATION is!!

Where is imagination? Dreams?

TOUCH
SPEECH SMELL TASTE HEARING
MEMORY SIGHT

were stories and they were magic. "Will you tell me a story tonight?" she asked.

"Which one would you like?"

"Something with faeries and magic," she said, then added, "and perhaps a dragon."

Which reminded the professor of what Bilgewallow had said after he had called mythology nonsense. "Too bad you chaps can't find a dragon or a dryad," Bilgewallow had snorted, amused at his own wit, "because it would take just such

an astounding miracle to save your department."

Remembering this, the professor began to mutter again. For a few moments he allowed himself to daydream about a ship that could take him to the lands of legend. Well, that kind of daydreaming sometimes results in the most surprising things, and this time that something was pure magic.

Hearing him talking to himself again, Miranda sighed. Cassandra, bored with how slowly they walked, jumped over a puddle and ran on ahead.

So it was she who first saw the odd little ship moored alongside an old, abandoned dock. There was something very strange and mysterious about the ship, and Cassandra thought immediately of magic. She called back to her father and sister, but they paid no attention.

Finally, the professor and Miranda walked to her side, and Cassandra, although she knew pointing wasn't polite, pointed at the ship and began asking

H.M.S. Basset

A mysteriously magical vessel that had even more surprises inside than out.

questions. Her father and sister could see that here was something quite extraordinary indeed.

The ship was small, delicate and seemingly decorated just for beauty rather than for a particular function. More surprising still, the crew members moving around the decks and rigging were barely more than three feet tall. Cassandra knew, because of all the stories her father had told her, that these were dwarves. Flashing here and there, however, sometimes nearly upsetting the dwarves, were even smaller creatures dressed in absurdly tall stovepipe hats, bright red jackets and spats. Cassandra pulled at her father's sleeve. "Daddy, who are *they*?"

Perplexed, the professor shook his head. He, too, recognized dwarves, but even though he knew what they were, he had never actually expected to see *one*, much less a ship full of them. Miranda turned to see if other passersby were looking, but they were all alone. "I think we should go home," she said nervously.

Suddenly one of the dwarves walked briskly to where they stood. With a short bow, he introduced himself as Malachi, Captain of H.M.S. *Basset*. Then this strange personage said something that Professor Aisling would never forget ever in his life.

"Your ship, Professor Aisling, is ready and at your bidding."

"My ship?" asked the professor.

"Aye, sir. And the tides of inspiration are with us, so you're right on time. Shall we board?"

The professor was completely flummoxed, which means to be confused and surprised all at once. When one has wished for a ship and then had the wish immediately granted, one is sure to be completely, perhaps even absolutely, flummoxed.

"I can't believe this!" the professor said, and the wonderment showed in his face.

"But, sir," Captain Malachi answered seriously, "we're here precisely because you *can* believe." Professor Aisling stared in amazement. He looked at the ship, then back at Miranda and Cassandra. "My daughters…" he said, "they're so young. They should be in school learning geometry, history, geography. They should—"

"Is that more important than the geography of imagination?" Captain Malachi broke in. "Or the geometry of inspiration? You are all part of the adventure." It was as strange as anything the professor had ever heard, and as ridiculous—and as impossible to refuse. He felt truly lighthearted for the first time in many months.

"Girls," he laughed gaily, "let's have an adventure!" Cassandra needed no urging. She cried, "Yes!" and fairly danced up the gangway. Miranda stood unmoving, a worried look on her face. "This isn't even my best dress," she said. "And…and… how long will we be gone?" The professor hadn't an answer, but Captain Malachi scratched his chin and replied, "If I'm not mistaken, all of yesterday and most of the day before."

The professor couldn't help but laugh merrily.

Dwarves and top-hatted gremlins make up the Basset's crew.

Archimedes

Eli

"Never mind," answered her father, patting Miranda's cheek. "I'll need you to help me to keep an eye on Cassandra." Miranda hung back a moment longer; then, with a sigh, she took her father's arm. They walked up the gangway and onto the magical little ship.

"Welcome aboard the *Basset*, Professor, ladies," Captain Malachi said with a neat, formal bow. "Here's First Mate Sebastian. He'll show you to your quarters and give you a tour of the ship, while the crew and I get us under way." With another nod of his head he turned and began call-ing orders: "Bosun Eli, weigh anchor! Helmsman Archimedes, hard alee! Seaman Augustus, raise the banner!"

As the Aislings watched, a beautiful, turquoise-blue, embroidered silk banner lifted into the grow-ing breeze. On it were the words *Credendo vides*. "*Credendo vides*," the professor said, hardly able to believe what he had read. "By believing, one sees."

"What nonsense!" said Miranda.

"Daddy?" asked Cassandra. "Isn't it supposed to be 'seeing is believing'?"

"Well," began the professor.

"It all depends, Miss, on how you look at it," answered Sebastian.

Captain Malachi Sebastian Augustus

[15]

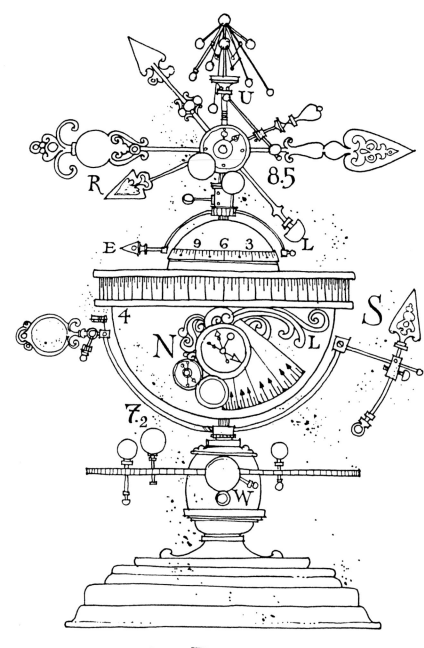

WUNTARLABE

If you want to go adventuring in the landscape of imagination, a wuntarlabe is just the thing to help you navigate the Otherwhere and Otherwhen.

There began around them a sudden flurry of activity. The *Basset*, which had seemed somewhat strange from a distance, was even stranger now that they were aboard. The dwarves went about their business, but the little people darted to and fro, in and out of the rigging.

"Excuse me, Mr. Sebastian, but what are those little people with the big hats and big feet?" asked Cassandra. Miranda and the professor each considered shushing her but were equally curious.

"The little people are gremlins, Miss."

"Are they trying to help?" she asked.

"Yes, Miss. Sometimes they find a short way or a better way to do something—and other times we spend an hour or two sorting out the mess. But among our folk there's an old saying, 'Use a dwarf to set the *wuntarlabe* and a gremlin to spin its wheel.' So we need them, though often enough it's like needing a headache."

"What's a winterlube?" Cassandra demanded.

"No," he corrected, "it's said *woonterlob* or, if you're very, very proper, *voonterlob*."

"Well, what is it?" she asked.

"A wuntarlabe is a device that we use to find the way out of the sensible world and navigate within the landscape of imagination. Come this way and we can watch it work."

As they sailed toward open ocean, Captain Malachi gave the order for Helmsman Archimedes and a fidgety gremlin to work the wuntarlabe. Archimedes took their sensible position, set the gears, and then stood back. The gremlin, whose top hat was pulled so far down they could not see his eyes, grinned as he climbed onto a stool. He put his sticky little forefinger into a depression in the silver and copper wheel and, with complete abandon, whirled it howsoever it would go.

The wheel began to twirl and the dials whirled.

Dials pointed up, down and every which
way. Bells dinged and tinkled from within,
and the entire wuntarlabe plunked, jingled
and sparkled. It vibrated and whirred. Then,
with a loud PING! and two THOCKS! and
a CLICK! it pointed authoritatively with
its grandest and most bejeweled
arrow—*THAT WAY*!

"What nonsense!" Miranda said, for
the deep blue water looked just the same.

"Of course," said Sebastian. "You'll
never find magic by being sensible.
Shall we go below?"

*The Basset's motto was
"Credendo vides," the Latin
for "By believing,
one sees."*

Cassandra was the first to go. As she drew beneath the deck, down to where she could see the space below, she gasped, "Good gracious!" and her head popped back above the deck. Then she ducked down again. Laughing delightedly, she clattered down the steps and called back over her shoulder, "Come along; it's lovely!"

The professor followed, doing much the same, though as he stooped to look below for the second time, his face was full of wonder. He looked up at Miranda and Sebastian and said in amazement, "It doesn't fit!" Then he, too, disappeared from sight.

Miranda descended slowly, worrying that they were playing some sort of jest. She stepped down and down until she could see her father and sister walking in a great hall. She too popped back up to look again at the small deck of the *Basset*. Then she stepped down for another look at the grand but surely impossible room below. Looking back at Sebastian, as though this were somehow his fault, she pointed below.

[18]

"That cannot possibly be there. It doesn't work. The room is simply far too large to be inside this tiny ship!" cried Miranda.

The normally serious Sebastian gave a tiny smile, and his eyes twinkled.

"As you said, Miss Miranda, it's all nonsense."

Sebastian, still smiling, politely led Miranda to her cabin. It was a pretty little room, but its beauty was lost on Miranda. She soon scurried back above. Her father and sister were happily exploring the strange space below, but Miranda didn't like it. The whole thing was absurd; there had to be some other, and more reasonable, explanation.

Leaving London for the lands of legend, the small ship slipped silently out to sea.

She walked toward the bow of the ship, while a soft breeze cooled her face. Suddenly, looking up at the sails billowing forward, she realized that the wind was coming in the wrong direction. The banner with its ridiculous motto flew with the wind, in the opposite direction of the sails. It seemed to her that the strange little ship was merely pretending to do what a ship would do. "Doesn't anything work the way it's supposed to here?" she muttered unhappily, and not for the last time.

[19]

Dwarves

Dwarves are orderly and methodical and much prefer to know how they're going to do something before they actually start. The oldest tales (which probably originated in Germany) of these folk tell of a race clever with tools and forge-work. They were renowned for making gold rings and iron crowns. Originally mountain dwellers, dwarves created marvelous underground towns and fortresses. The Basset's dwarves have an even stranger homeland.

Gremlins

Over the centuries, the creatures we call gremlins have been called by many names, not all of them complimentary. Child of Chaos, Little Mischief, and Fortune's Other Baby are but a few. Despite such names, gremlins aren't malicious. They're spontaneous, and curious about everything, which at some times leads to fortunate discoveries and at others to very large messes. Gremlins are forever picking up things and putting them in their hats.

Unlike her sister, Miranda was not amused to discover that the Basset was bigger below decks than above.

In the days that followed, Cassandra and the professor discovered much about their vessel. On deck, the ship was small and full of efficient toil by dwarves and rampant activity by gremlins. Below was an endless series of staterooms, dining rooms, galleys, storerooms and a library that Professor Aisling could not believe existed anywhere outside of a university.

Cassandra became friends with First Mate Sebastian almost at once. She was taller than he, and this made her feel that she was quite grown-up. Although he was very old, Sebastian listened seriously to everything Cassandra said to him. He answered her questions and told her stories about dwarves in ancient days.

When Sebastian was busy with seaman's duties, Cassandra and her father wandered in the strange, impossibly large spaces below deck, calling out to each other to come look here or there.

Only Miranda seemed less than enchanted with her surroundings. She walked the decks or fussed about in her quarters, but she would not explore. "It's all too silly," she told herself, "the kind of stuff a child would believe." She couldn't admit that she found it confusing, maybe even a little frightening. Instead, she said to herself, "I'm waiting for the real answer."

ne morning Cassandra woke to the sound of Seaman Augustus shouting, "Land ho!" followed by Captain Malachi's order to steer toward the shoreline. She fairly catapulted out of bed, leapt into her dress and jumped into her shoes. Her father came out of his room nearly as quickly. Miranda followed more slowly, fretting over a bit of hem that had come undone.

Once ashore, dwarves and gremlins filled casks from a stream spilling into the bay. Cassandra's father walked up the beach, following the narrow strip of sand to where a cliff blocked the way, but Cassandra was drawn to the forest's edge. She could hear unfamiliar birds and strained to see what they looked like. Suddenly she saw a light flit past not ten feet into the forest, and then, just as suddenly, it was gone.

"Good gracious!" she said and turned toward her sister. "Miranda! I saw something!" Miranda sat on a bit of driftwood inspecting her sleeve cuffs. Without looking up, Miranda replied, "What was it?"

"I don't know. It seemed to be a sort of light, like a little star that moved."

"Oh, Cassandra, don't be silly. It was just a firefly."

"No, it wasn't!" Cassandra retorted, and again saw the light in the forest. "There!" she shouted and dashed into the woods after it.

At first landfall, an ancient legend and a mystery awaited the travelers.

"Cassandra, come back this instant! You cannot go into the forest by yourself." Miranda turned toward their father and called, "Father, Cassandra said she saw something in the for—"

"A light?" he asked excitedly, for he had seen it, too. "A flickering little light?"

Captain Malachi turned just in time to see the professor and Miranda disappear into the forest. With a quick command, he urged his crew to follow. Before long, all of them (except Miranda, who simply wouldn't look) were catching glimpses of the dancing lights, always ahead, always drawing them on, deeper and deeper into the forest. They followed an old trail along a stream, which became ever noisier and more boisterous. Soon they began to hear the roar of falling water.

They rounded a bend in the trail, and before them a waterfall tumbled down the sheer face of a cliff. Straight toward the roaring cascade the dancing lights flew. Wheeling suddenly, they flashed behind the curtain of water. For several minutes, the travelers waited for their return, but the dancing lights did not reappear.

[26]

Cassandra looked up at her father, but he was as stumped as she. With a quiet little "Hmmm," Captain Malachi walked to the waterfall. He leaned toward the cascade and peered beyond it. "I think there may be something back there," he shouted over the roar of the falls. "Maybe a cave. There's a broad ledge going in."

There was indeed something—a passageway fading to darkness. They made a simple torch with a pine branch, and the professor, who was the tallest of the travelers, held it aloft as they entered. Cassandra took her father's free hand because it was really quite dark, and a little frightening. No one spoke, and even their footsteps seemed muffled. Suddenly a thundering roar from the blackest part of the cavern shattered the eerie silence.

Suddenly, the dancing lights disappeared behind the falls.

"Who dares enter the realm of the king?" asked a voice like fifty rusty hinges. The professor hastily pushed his daughters behind him, as the fabled Manticore glared and lashed his scorpion-spined tail. Beads of sweat broke out on the professor's forehead. He took a deep breath.

"Do I have the honor," he began in his politest manner, "of addressing the renowned and mighty Manticore, most recently of Ancient Greece and Asia Minor?"

"Huff," the Manticore replied, drawing himself to his proudest height. "And India and Persia, I might add," he said, still stretching his wings and showing a great many teeth. "To say nothing of being universally feared."

"You are indeed a formidable creature, and, er, we do most humbly beg your pardon for intruding without invitation upon your rest," answered the professor. "We ask only that we may pass through your chamber—"

"No one may pass without express permission from the king."

"The king?"

"The king."

"Perhaps—"

"There is no perhaps," replied the Manticore with great finality. "Although it has been something of a pleasure to make your brief acquaintance, it is my obligation to dispatch those who enter the realm of the king without permission."

"What?" cried Cassandra. "Dispatch? Doesn't that mean kill?"

"Hush, Cassandra," whispered her father.

"But it's not nice to kill people!" she cried. "Not nice at all!"

"Nice?" said the Manticore, considering it. "No, the king said nothing of being nice, only of dispatching intruders. Therefore, it is my sworn duty to—"

At that moment, in flew the dancing lights, flitting around the Manticore's great head. Cassandra gasped, for against the dark backdrop of the cavern the dancing lights could be clearly seen to be tiny winged people—*faeries*!

THE MANTICORE

From Topsell's Historie of Fowre-footed Beastes, 1607

A fearsome winged creature having a lion's body and mane, but a manlike face. His three rows of teeth, spiked tail and grumpy demeanor helped strike terror amongst the people of many ancient cultures.

The faeries' quick movements seemed to confuse the Manticore, who turned just as a faerie darted close to his head, and the little creature flew right into his ear. With a great shake and a snuffling, sneezy sound, the Manticore shook his head and the little faerie went tumbling, wing over elbow, and nearly hit the wall. But the faeries flew to the old monster again and whispered something.

This had an immediate effect on the Manticore. He lay down on his rocky shelf and waved a paw in their direction. "Upon further consideration," he said with a sigh, "I have decided that you may pass." With a sidelong glance at the faeries, he muttered "Harrumph," and turned to face the wall. Now the explorers could see that his coat and wings were actually rather tattered and moth-eaten. Cassandra didn't know why, but she felt a bit sorry for the Manticore and wondered if he were ever lonely in his dark cave.

As they walked up out of the cavern and into another forest, Cassandra thought, "How odd." It had been a bit past midday when they walked behind the waterfall, and they had not been long in the Manticore's cave. "So why," Cassandra asked herself, "is twilight here already?" Walking on, they found themselves among tall trees and an ancient stone ruin, when she and the other travelers heard music.

Before them had just appeared a faerie woman, around whom several smaller faeries flitted on silent wings. The travelers stood captivated. As quietly as evening, the faerie woman moved among the fallen stones, and as though drawn forward by enchantment, the travelers followed.

A faerie woman walked silently through the ruin.

[30]

Among trees, under arches, around fallen walls she walked. Unhurriedly, the faerie woman passed behind one of the stone columns. Perhaps it was a trick of the waning day that made the last sight of her pale skirt flicker with silvery light as it disappeared behind the stone.

She did not reappear on the other side. For many moments, no one moved. Then one of the gremlins scurried round the stone column, and then ran round again. His astonishment was so complete that after he had run his second course, he stopped, removed his hat and sat down, FLUMP! on the ground. The professor and Malachi walked around the pillar themselves and were as confused as the gremlin. The faerie woman had disappeared, taking the remaining daylight with her.

One moment, Cassandra stood staring at the pillar; the next, she was overtaken by an irresistable drowsiness. "How strange this land is," she murmured. She sat down against one of the old stones and fell immediately asleep. Miranda intended to say, "Come along, Cassandra; this is no place to sleep," but could not stifle her yawns long enough to speak. Seconds later all the travelers were huddled near the wall, wrapped in slumber.

In a bright new morning, the sleepers were awakened by a joyful din and bustling activity.

Cassandra jumped up in wonder. Where there had been only a misty stone ruin the night before, there were now dancers, singers, jugglers and serving faeries with trays and baskets laden with ripe fruits and breads. "Oh! We've wakened right in the middle of a faerie story!" Cassandra shouted delightedly. She was used to hearing about faeries at bedtime, but it was much better, she decided, to wake up to them.

Miranda looked about suspiciously, not at all pleased. (Noticing this, Cassandra decided that being sixteen musn't be the *least* bit of fun.) Their father began to ask all sorts of questions. The serv-

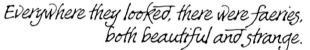
Everywhere they looked, there were faeries, both beautiful and strange.

ing faeries, giggling at his bewilderment, answered none. Instead, they laid a white cloth on the grass and set out a picnic feast, urging the wayfarers (who needed little prompting) to break their fast with this delicacy or that.

When the last wild berry had been hidden in one of the gremlins' hats (along with the last pair of rolls), a group of exceedingly well-dressed faeries bowed politely and asked the travelers to follow and be presented to King Oberon and Queen Titania.

Oberon, King of the Faeries

Titania, Queen of the Faeries

Although Oberon was probably originally a German legend, and his queen, Titania, was strictly from English faerie stories, they were in complete agreement that the Aislings were the most engaging mortals since Shakespeare.

Cassandra's eyes were wide as they approached the royal couple on the dais. "How splendid," she thought, "that Oberon and Titania look precisely as the king and queen of the faeries ought to look." At that moment, she found herself gazing into King Oberon's eyes and had the oddest sensation that the king knew what she was thinking. She blushed, afraid that she might have been rude, and made a very deep curtsey to show that she really was a well-brought-up little girl.

Beside her, Cassandra felt her father start. She looked up and saw that he, too, was surprised by King Oberon's strange gaze. Cassandra wondered what Miranda made of it all. She looked at her older sister, but Miranda just stood staring at the ground. "Why, she's missing everything!" thought Cassandra, and she wondered why one had to grow up and be serious.

Cassandra felt a light touch on her shoulder. She turned to see Queen Titania smiling down at her and instantly thought of her mother, though she wasn't sure why. Then the queen gently touched Miranda's wrist. "Will you walk with me?" Titania asked the sisters. That was fine with Miranda, who found the king's eyes awfully strange. Cassandra was awed by the king, but when a queen calls, one goes. They walked away as their father politely said, "Your Majesty."

[36]

"It seems you've gotten the voyage you dreamed of, Professor Aisling," answered the king.

"Yes, Your Majesty. But I don't understand; how is it that I . . . ?" He trailed off.

"*Credendo vides*, Professor. By believing, one sees," said the king.

"I believe, Your Majesty, but what am I to do?" asked the professor. Oberon smiled.

"When good Malachi asked you aboard the *Basset*, why did you go?" he asked.

"Because I had wished for it, and suddenly there it was, like magic. And because I want the chance to show that what I teach, what I do, is important," said the professor.

"Are we important?"

"Oh, yes, Your Majesty. Legends offer mystery and romance and beauty and adventure to anyone who cares to find out about them. To lose the old stories . . . I cannot bear to think of a world without them."

"This, then, is your quest, Professor: to keep open the doorway between our worlds."

Oberon gives Aisling his quest.

While the king and the professor talked, the queen walked with the girls to a quiet place apart. The queen took Cassandra's hand in hers.

"Tell me about your mother," Titania said softly. Cassandra's eyes instantly swam with tears, and she could not answer.

"She was taken from us," Miranda replied, swallowing hard. "Not quite a year ago." She shook her head and fell silent.

"I wish she could come back," Cassandra said, looking up into Titania's wise, kindly eyes. "Sometimes, when I'm just falling asleep, I forget and I think she might come in and say good night to me."

"Perhaps she does, in her own way," Titania said firmly. "When someone loves us very much, she goes on loving us always, and a little thing like death is not likely to get in the way."

"That's rather like what Daddy told me," said Cassandra, wiping her eyes.

"Yes? What did he say?" asked the queen.

"He said that she would be our guardian angel now that she isn't able to be our mother."

"I'm sure he's right."

"Are you, Queen Titania? Do you really and truly think so; it's not just a thing to say because I'm not grown-up yet?"

"Yes, I do mean it, really and truly, Cassandra." Titania smiled and stroked her hair.

"She always took care of us when we were ill," Miranda whispered, with a look of intense sorrow. "And we always got better. But when we tried to take care of her, it didn't work. And *I* never see her when I'm falling asleep, and whenever I think of her, she's just . . . gone. Lost."

"Ah, Miranda, sweet child, your mother isn't lost," the queen replied kindly. "She's as near as your next heartbeat. You just need to learn where to look." She drew an ornate little box from the folds of her dress and held it out to Miranda. "This may be of some help when the time comes." Miranda slowly reached out and took the box. "Thank you, Your Majesty," she said, giving a little curtsey. "Do you wish me to open it now?" "I wish," answered the queen,

"that *you* should choose the time of its opening, my dear."

Miranda looked at the tiny box, then hesitantly slid it into her pocket. Queen Titania turned back to Cassandra and said, "For you, dear Cassandra, since you are already aware of angels, a talisman of their care when you need it." From around her own neck she drew a gold chain on which hung a polished stone.

"For me? Thank you, Your Majesty!"

"You are really and truly welcome, Cassandra." As Cassandra clasped the pretty stone, she looked up at Titania in surprise. The stone lay warm in her hand, and as she held it she could feel within it a tiny, rhythmic beat.

As they walked back toward where the professor stood with the king, Titania caught a look of such deep sorrow on Miranda's face that she said, "My dear, you are so sad. Is there nothing at all in the Court of the Faeries to make you smile?"

Miranda bit her lip and curtsied. "Please, Your Majesty, I would like a needle and thread with which to mend my dress."

"My poor darling! We could dress you up in faerie robes of any color you choose," the queen said. Miranda wanted to cry out, "But this is all I have from home!" yet she couldn't be impolite. She stared at her toes and curtsied instead.

Titania offered comfort . . . and gave secret gifts.

[39]

The next morning, as they prepared to leave, King Oberon told them, "I think you should take the old Manticore with you. He's been too long in that dark cavern, and I think a sea voyage would be good for his old bones."

"Excuse me, Your Majesty," Cassandra asked politely, "but will he bite?"

self to his full height. He raised an eyebrow and stared down his nose at the *Basset*'s crew.

"But if you'd rather not—" said the king.

"No, no," said the Manticore hastily. "You're right. Someone who knows what he's about needs to keep an eye on this lot."

Titania gathered Cassandra into her arms and

Oberon urged the old Manticore
to accompany the travelers.

"I think you'll find that he has noble restraint, if a somewhat rough manner," said the king, smiling.

"Old friend," Oberon said when the Manticore had joined them, "there's not as much to guarding the realm of the king as there once was, and I think your excellent help is much needed aboard the *Basset*. I would like to commission you to accompany them, since they will need someone with both bravery and good sense."

"Hmph," snorted the Manticore. He drew him-

kissed her cheek. Cassandra wished that the queen instead of the Manticore were to go with them, but she didn't say so. Titania then gave Miranda a bit of cloth in which lay a needle and some thread. Miranda cried, "Oh! Thank you, Your Majesty," and curtsied deeply.

As they walked out of the faeries' encampment, Cassandra told her father with a sigh, "I expect that I shall become very tired of watching Miranda mend her dress."

Some faeries are preoccupied with elaborate dress and decoration, while others take no thought for clothing and seem to be dressed in cobwebs.

The air is always alive with delightful little creatures no bigger than my thumb.

Some are winged and lovely; others are charmingly odd-visaged!!

FAERIES!

More magical than I had dreamed, and more varied. Some are as small as flowers, some as tall as I, and all sizes between. But all seem to exist as a celebration of nature's enchantment. They make use of the ancient ruin not as humans would, by placing new buildings upon the old stones, but, like the lilies of the field, they bloom where they are, enlivening the landscape merely by their presence.

assandra stood between her father and Sebastian as Archimedes set the wuntarlabe. She slipped one hand into her father's and then took Sebastian's with the other. The old dwarf looked up with surprise; then he smiled and squeezed her hand. Miranda, as Cassandra had predicted, sat fussing with hems and seams and ignoring all else.

Their next landfall was a small island with a sandy beach. Since it was close to lunchtime, they decided to picnic there. Filling their cups and plates, the travelers had just set to their meal when a scream like that of a family of furious falcons tore out of the sky and three huge, hurtling birds swooped and fluttered among the picnickers.

Except that they weren't birds. The travelers did indeed see feathers, wings and bony bird-feet, but the faces of these creatures had noses and lips rather than beaks. They had long hair piled not awfully neatly on their heads. The

Picnic raiders far worse than ants

professor gasped in delight as the three "ladies" landed amidst their lunch.

Suddenly, one of them snatched a roll from Augustus, who cried out, "Here now! What's this?" Then all three began snatching this, that and the other tasty thing from any plate within reach. One stole Cassandra's bread and butter, but when another grabbed her apple, she cried, "Oh no, you don't!" and grabbed it right back. The harpies hopped and fluttered over the sand and continued to steal from any plate they could. Soon the picnic became more of a melee than a meal.

"They're harpies!" yelled the professor to his companions, which had absolutely no effect on the uproar. A harpy grabbed his plate and ate everything on it.

[43]

Everywhere, the three harpies swooped and grabbed and swallowed, but Captain Malachi had had enough. He barked an order and two of the harpies were caught. The third nearly escaped, but as she lifted off, the Manticore plopped a huge paw on her tail.

"Aiee!" screeched one. "You call that a feast?"

"Aiee!" squawked another. "Sweetmeats! And where are the sugar cakes?"

"Aiee!" cried the third. "Not fair! Not fair! They always get the most!"

"You got my joint of beef," said the Manticore, who held her firmly and leaned down eye to eye with her. He roared loudly enough to make her jump and snapped his jaws together a feather's breadth from her nose.

At last there was quiet. The travelers brushed off their clothes, and the harpies shook crumbs out of their feathers.

"Ladies," the professor began, "we are happy to make your acquaintance—"

"Hmph!" said the Manticore.

"Is there more food?" one of the harpies asked hopefully.

"You're really still hungry?" the professor asked in amazement.

"She's not as hungry as I am!" cried another.

"What about me?" screamed the last. "I haven't had a good meal in years—no thanks to you two!"

Harpies

They love food and have developed a passion for cooking!

Sent by the Greek gods, these woman-headed birds tormented King Phineus of Salmydessus by stealing and fouling his food.

"Aiee! Aiee! Aiee!" the harpies began shrieking at each other. The travelers all put their fingers in their ears. Finally the professor shouted:

"THERE'S MORE FOOD!"

"Where?" and "Bring it on!" and "Now you're talking!" they said, more or less simultaneously. Another picnic was quickly organized and laid out again on the sand. Once they had actually been offered food, the harpies were more polite in their habits. The professor asked them to tell something of their lives on the island.

"Not much to tell," said the eldest harpy. "Never enough food, since nobody asks for our services much. Who remembers to invite us to feasts these days, I ask you?"

Nodding, the other two harpies looked sadly at their bony feet and sighed their peculiar, "Aiee, nobody." Cassandra had to smile, for this was precisely how one of her schoolmates, Priscilla Poole, talked so that people would feel sorry for her and invite her to tea.

Professor Aisling began telling them about the voyage and its purpose, but all three interrupted with, "We know, we know; we want to come, too!" He asked how they knew of it, but in their great delight they drowned out the question. "A voyage!" they crowed. "Galleys and pantries and larders," they chirped. "Soups and stews and pastries and cakes!" they warbled.

"Father!" Miranda cried. "You cannot expect us to travel with those . . . those *horrid* creatures. Look at them! Did you see how they ate?"

"Why, Miranda, are you finally taking an interest in our voyage?" the professor asked teasingly. Miranda frowned and crossed her arms.

"Father, they're odious. That wretched, tattered old monster is bad enough, but this!" The professor became serious and said softly, "Miranda, *we're*

It's never wise to fool with the Manticore's lunch.

the strangers here, and what seems so horrid may merely be new to your eyes. Perhaps if we give it a little time—"

"Time! What about the time we've been wandering around here? What are our friends at home thinking? Without even a word to anyone, without packing, without anything, we go sailing off in an impossible ship on this absurd adventure." She looked at him with tear-filled eyes. "I just want to go home." She turned away.

Cassandra couldn't understand her sister's unhappiness. So far they had had simply amazing adventures. Cassandra tugged at her father's hand. "*I* don't want to go home."

THE SPHINX

The Sphinx has a human head and arms, eagle's wings, and the hind legs and tail of a great cat.

One-time terror along the road to Thebes. Failure to solve her riddle led to the demise of many a traveler until Oedipus was able to answer it correctly.

after a sketch by MOREAU

A distant relative may still reside in the Egyptian desert.

THE SPHINX'S RIDDLE: What animal is that which in the morning goes on four legs, at noon on two, and in the evening upon three?

After lunch, they followed an old stone road through dry, sandy wasteland that soon gave way to huge rock formations. The landscape was so still and empty that they nearly missed the most extraordinary figure sitting immobile, high above them among the weathered rocks and boulders.

With the head and torso of a woman, dark wings, and the lower body of a great cat, she sat as if long years had left her unable to move. The travelers stood directly below her, but she didn't acknowledge their presence. The old Manticore made a strange sound, and only then did she begin to turn, very slowly, looking first at the Manticore and then at the professor.

"Greetings, fair lady," he said softly. The Sphinx seemed somehow to be struggling for voice as she continued to gaze into his eyes. Finally she spoke.

"Greetings, mortal." Her voice was deep and husky, as if she had not used it for many years, or perhaps centuries. "You are the wayfarer who goes in search of the old myths," she said.

"Yes, madam. Professor Algernon Aisling at your service. But, fair lady," he asked with a puzzled frown, remembering his earlier question of the harpies, "how do you know of our quest?" She simply turned away.

The professor then asked the Sphinx to accompany them, telling her that Oberon had charged him with keeping alive the legends and myths.

"But I cannot go," the Sphinx said, "for my riddle is broken. What use is the Sphinx without a riddle?" she asked with despair.

The Manticore cleared his throat. "Excuse me," he said. "I don't know a great deal about riddle-making, but I expect it's about wise sayings and knowing a great many things." The Sphinx nodded that this was true. "Well, then," he said, "the place to go about making a new riddle is a library."

"Yes!" cried the professor. "What my friend the Manticore means is that aboard the *Basset* is a huge library. I have never before seen the like."

The Sphinx looked back and forth between the professor and the Manticore but remained immobile, as if unable to come to a decision. The harpies had been quiet, but this was too much.

"What, you got something a lot better to do?"

screamed one, indignantly ruffling her feathers.

"Got a long to-do list today, Sphinx?" shrieked the second.

"Come on, come *on*," screeched the third. "It's nearly dinnertime!"

"Ladies, please," said the professor. The Sphinx, however, waved a languid hand as if to say, "What can you expect of harpies?" She leapt gracefully down from her perch among the rocks and, without more ado, accompanied them back to the *Basset*.

Sea travel with the harpies was…interesting. They took over the galley, and Cassandra often went there to listen to them argue, for they never, ever agreed on a recipe. All in all, Cassandra found their cooking to be quite good, except that there were pinfeathers in the soup rather more often than she would have liked.

Cassandra had the most fun, however, watching the Manticore and the Sphinx. Although the two never spoke and were always some distance apart, Cassandra watched them glance casually at each other every now and again.

"Look now, Sebastian," she whispered. "See them look at each other and pretend that it's an accident? And they are rather alike. Do you suppose they might fall in love?"

"I wouldn't venture to guess, Miss Cassandra," her friend replied.

"Well, I would," she said firmly. "I think they will. You must have heard, Sebastian, that in all the best adventures, someone falls in love."

Alone no longer, the creatures of myth awoke to the joys of companionship.

ot many days thereafter, they came into view of another island, upon which lay a rambling stone city. Excitedly, the professor watched the shore approach as the dwarves and gremlins prepared for another expedition. Cassandra, happy as much for a change of scenery as for the adventure, combed her hair, put an apple in her pocket and declared herself ready to go.

Professor Aisling went to gather the rest of the group. He found the harpies deep in a discussion about cake, and the air was thick with flour and pinfeathers (which, the professor thought, didn't bode well for the cake). Not unexpectedly, the harpies declined to accompany him, as did the Manticore and the Sphinx when they were asked.

Hearing that the Manticore, the Sphinx and all three harpies were to stay aboard, Miranda was only too ready to accompany her father and sister.

Once ashore, they found that the city was not merely empty, but in ruins. They walked through passages and thoroughfares that must at one time have been very beautiful, but were now silent and covered with the dust of ages. Here and there were the pale remains of murals and frescoes, and at one of these the professor stopped, surprised.

Brushing away an accumulation of dust and grit, he uncovered a painting of a dancing figure leaping over a charging bull. Over his shoulder he called excitedly, "Come and look at this!" When everyone had drawn near, he pointed to the leaping dancer. "I think this figure was part of a painting of the bull-dancers from the court of King Minos. If I'm right, we may find a labyrinth nearby."

Cassandra loved the maze gardens of London, and a labyrinth, her father had told her, was like a maze garden. It was bigger, of course, and built of stone, not shrubbery. So when they discovered

a long passageway wherein were many doors and intersecting corridors, Cassandra ran inside straightaway. Her father quickly called her back.

"I want to go inside, too, pet," he said, "but if it's a labyrinth, we must take care that we are able to find our way out. I wish I had thought to bring a ball of string." Cassandra checked her pocket but found only the apple she'd put there earlier. Miranda had a little pocket mirror and, of course, the needle and thread, but not nearly enough thread.

One of the gremlins jabbered at them and began to empty his hat. In quick succession he pulled out a bottle, two apples, a muffin, several marbles, a horseshoe, three seashells, a bagpipe and finally, with a little chirp of triumph, out came a ball of bright red string. Grinning proudly, he held it out to the professor.

"Why, thank you, old chap! I shall never cease to be amazed by the incredible array of whatnots you fellows have squirreled away in those hats," the professor said, taking the string. "Now let's all keep together."

They began to explore the ancient, uninhabited island city of King Minos.

Paying out string, they moved into the corridor. Cleverly placed windows allowed light into the depths, illuminating a mysterious space. Walls and passages and stairs showed through various doorways, but many of them looked not quite right.

"How strange," Cassandra murmured. "That stair looks as if it cannot lead one anywhere." Walking on, she saw to her left a little opening—not a door, for it was too short and also several inches off the ground. It was like a small, low window. Curious, she climbed through, and in only a few steps she was far enough from her companions that she could hear nothing of their footsteps or their voices. Soon she was even more completely confused about her directions than before.

Suddenly, Cassandra heard something. "Daddy?" she called out, and her voice quavered. There was no answer, but still there was something, perhaps the sound of footsteps. She crept around the next bend and then stopped with a little gasp.

King Minos, legendary ruler of the isle of Crete, commanded the architect Daedelus to design a labyrinth to imprison something sinister.

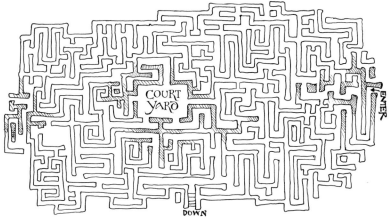

In front of her stood the Minotaur. She knew from her father's stories that he was quite horrible, and it was much too much for a little girl who was only nine years and eleven months old. Cassandra covered her face with her hands and began to cry.

But something quite strange happened then. Under her gown, she could feel a growing warmth in Titania's stone. It made her feel as if she were not so terribly alone. Without opening her eyes, she drew it out and held it in her hand. She took a deep breath and then opened her eyes. The Minotaur took an ominous step toward her.

"I'm lost," Cassandra said in a small voice. "Can you help me?" The Minotaur stopped in slow surprise. He stood immobile for some time, thinking.

"Nooooo," he answered, sounding rather like a sad cow. "I'm lost, too."

"You're lost?" she asked. He nodded his head.

"How long have you been here?"

"Looonng time," he answered. He made a mournful mooing sound, and instantly Cassandra was full of pity. He seemed so helpless, and not so very intelligent.

"You must be awfully hungry," she said. She offered him the apple from her pocket and took his hand. "Maybe we can find a way out together."

"There is no way out," he said with finality.

"You mean in all these years and years and years you couldn't find it?"

"I didn't look."

"Then how do you know there's no way out?" she asked.

"Daedalus said so. He built this place, and he told me there was no way out. So," he concluded sadly, "there's no way out."

"But," Cassandra pointed out, "if I found my way in, then *of course* there must be a way out." The Minotaur stopped (literally) to think.

"Do you mean that you can use a way in as a way out?" he asked. His brow was terribly furrowed with the effort.

"But of course you can," she replied.

"And it's all right?" he asked anxiously. "Isn't there a rule?"

Cassandra laughed merrily, squeezed his hand and pulled him forward. "Well, if there is, we shall break it into little bits."

Enormous figure, part man, part bull, with a wholly bad reputation.

There wasn't a labyrinth on the Basset, so the Minotaur made do with a closet.

So! By being just as brave and clever as she was kind and polite, Cassandra got out of an unpleasant situation and made a fine new friend as well. In a quite far away corridor of the labyrinth, however, poor Professor Aisling didn't know that Cassandra was safe. He was scared right out of his wits.

When the professor found Cassandra gone from the group, he paled. He knew what monstrous being prowled that strange space. It was as if a cold wind blew across the back of his neck. In a panic, he began to shout Cassandra's name and would have rushed down any old corridor if Miranda hadn't grasped his arm.

"Please, Father, we cannot have you lost, too," she said, which proves that Miranda, though she might fuss over her dress, could at the least keep her wits about her. Professor Aisling drew in a deep breath. He forced himself to be calm. All the travelers clustered together and began to move hastily down passageways, calling Cassandra's name. Guided by the Minotaur's fine, large ears, Cassandra was soon close enough to hear her friends shouting for her.

Over their own echoing shouts, they did not hear her calling back. But then they saw her round a corner and run straight into her father. He was so overjoyed that he swept her up in his arms and never even noticed the great beast who followed more shyly in her wake. Everyone else, however, had shrunk back against the wall in fright. Cassandra lifted her head from her father's shoulder.

"Daddy, look who I found! Can we take him with us?" Then, leaning close to her father's ear, she whispered, "He's not awfully clever, Daddy, and he'll never find his way out by himself."

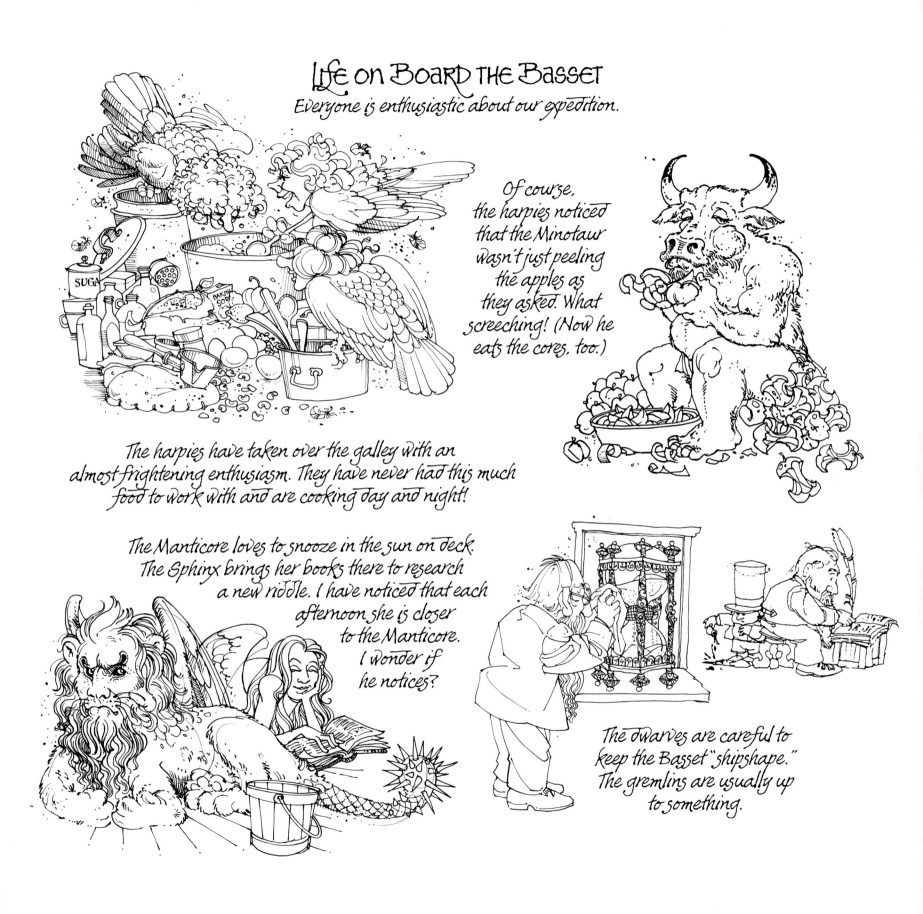

Life on Board the Basset

Everyone is enthusiastic about our expedition.

Of course, the harpies noticed that the Minotaur wasn't just peeling the apples as they asked. What screeching! (Now he eats the cores, too.)

The harpies have taken over the galley with an almost frightening enthusiasm. They have never had this much food to work with and are cooking day and night!

The Manticore loves to snooze in the sun on deck. The Sphinx brings her books there to research a new riddle. I have noticed that each afternoon she is closer to the Manticore. I wonder if he notices?

The dwarves are careful to keep the Basset "shipshape." The gremlins are usually up to something.

he day that they sailed into the fog, Cassandra was standing on deck near where Sebastian was working. As he worked, he told her the story of the Battle of Glettinflingle, which began when King Arnulf sneezed three times (a very bad omen) at King Worflieg's wedding. He had just gotten to the part where the two dwarf kings threw iron axes at each other and missed, when the professor, standing near the bow, peered over the water and said, "Fog!"

Well! He had scarcely said the word when the dense, swirling mist enveloped the *Basset*. Cassandra, who had seen many thick fogs in London, thought this one might win a contest as the foggiest of fogs. She could barely make out Sebastian's form a few feet away. Her father and the rest of the *Basset*'s crew were invisible.

There was the briefest break in the mist and all of them saw alongside, far too near for safety, huge jutting rocks. Captain Malachi called out an order to drop anchor. The *Basset* slowed, then halted, and the mist closed over them again.

Around them were only the creaking sounds of wooden timbers, the flap of sails and rope and the quiet swish of the waves. The shouts of the seamen and the professor sounded eerie and strange (and frightening) to Cassandra. Then she heard something far out in the fog.

"Singing!" said Cassandra to Sebastian. "Who could it be?" Suddenly she was trembling with dread and wanted her father. Holding the rail with one hand, Cassandra began walking toward the sound of her father's voice.

"Wait," said Sebastian. "Let's go together." He took her other hand and they walked carefully forward. Just as they had come close enough to make out the professor's form, there was a solid BUMP! against the ship, and Cassandra stumbled.

"What was that?" everyone cried out together. Dwarves leaned over the side to see if they'd hit a rock. Soon everyone heard the strange singing, coming eerily through the fog. They heard a metallic THUNK! and a CLANK! Then, slowly at first, but with growing speed, the anchor chain began to pay out and the *Basset*, willy-nilly, began to move. Before they had time to consider what strange thing could be pulling on the anchor, they were coursing past ominous rocks that rose from the waves like huge, horrid teeth.

What could possibly
be big enough
to drag the Basset?

MERMAIDS

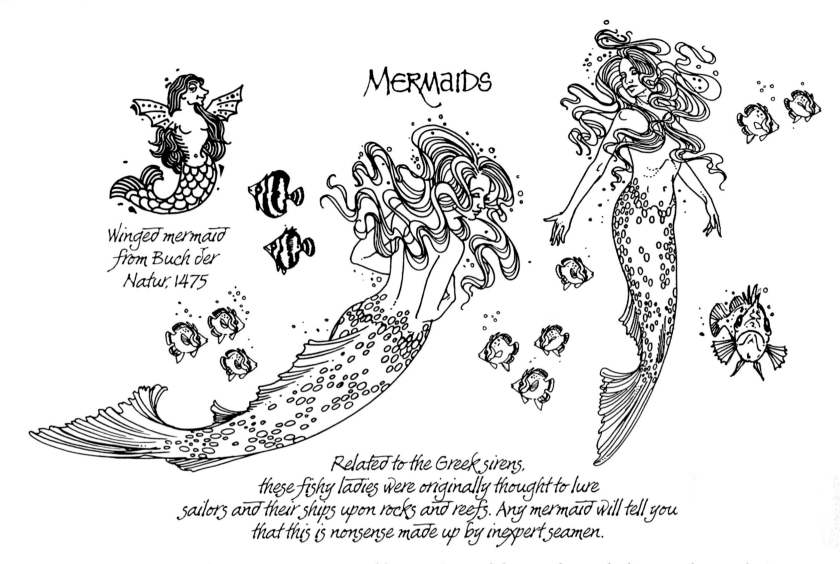

Winged mermaid from Buch der Natur, 1475

Related to the Greek sirens, these fishy ladies were originally thought to lure sailors and their ships upon rocks and reefs. Any mermaid will tell you that this is nonsense made up by inexpert seamen.

Although the perilous journey was not of long duration, it seemed to last hours. And then it was over as suddenly and inexplicably as it had begun. Once more the anchor held them firmly in place. Slowly the fog began to dissipate, and through the remaining tendrils of mist, the travelers heard soft, feminine laughter from the water below them.

Finally the last pale fingers of fog disappeared, and they found themselves in a placid lagoon off a sun-drenched tropical island. Even from the *Basset*'s deck, they could hear the call of birds. Beyond an expanse of golden beach was a lush forest of brilliantly colored flowers and lofty trees. Even Miranda sighed happily, and everyone was in much haste to lower the boats and go exploring.

As the dwarves unknotted knots and paid out rope, the travelers again heard giggles and tinkling laughter from the water below. Looking toward the sounds, they saw several lovely beings, not quite fish, not quite women. Below them swam another shape, a huge, sinuous, saurian shape: undoubtedly a sea serpent.

"Ladies," the professor called down, though he kept his voice rather stern, "we bid you good afternoon." A chorus of cheerful hellos and good days greeted him, along with more giggles.

"Welcome to the mermaid isle," called one of the beauties as her sisters laughed.

Sea Serpents, Coral Faeries, Flying Frogs

Apparently the mermaids are correct. The island is uninhabited by any but small creatures. Although this little isle is as beautiful as one could wish, the rocks that surround it make it difficult to reach.

The sea serpent does indeed heed the mermaids' singing, but that seems to be his only talent, for he is easily distracted.

"Strange welcome, madame, when your singing was likely meant to dash our vessel upon the rocks," began the professor.

"My good man, to whatever are you referring?" one asked with a momentary but not altogether successful attempt at gravity.

"Then why were you singing in the fog?"

"Well, how do *you* call a sea serpent?" one of the mermaids returned.

"But *why* would one call a sea serpent?"

"Well, how do you think your silly boat made it around all those jagged rocks? And what would we want with a ship?" they asked. "We have the whole ocean." They laughed heartily at the idea of riding a box on top of the water instead of swimming as any sensible creature would.

Suddenly, with a great shower of water, the sea serpent rose from the waves to where it could look

But it is the *Rana aeria* (as I have named them) that make me wish I could see this place studied in depth. Surely no other place on earth has these flying frogs! As their discoverer, I might be regarded differently.

•

Cassandra told me about the coral faeries along the reef. I sat for hours to see them, for they are shy and wary (not surprising, since they are tiny and the larger fish are always hungry), but what a reward! They are patterned and colored like the fish with which they swim.

the travelers in the eye. Then, with a great splash, it sank back into the waves and swam around the mermaids like a large, wet pet.

So the mystery was explained. During the fog, the sea serpent had pulled the *Basset* through the lethal rocks. The wayfarers found out that although the mermaids always sang to call the serpent, he was sometimes too far away and not quick enough to save boats in peril.

The sea serpent rose level with the ship again and turned its blue-green eyes to Cassandra, whose fair hair was not unlike the mermaids' sunny tresses.

"Daddy, can I pet him?" Cassandra asked.

"Well, now…" the professor began, but the creature subsided once more into the water. Professor Aisling gave a small sigh of relief. It is one thing to look a sea serpent in the eye and quite another to let your youngest child pat its nose.

[63]

Aisling made notes and drawings in his journal. The Sphinx and the Manticore moved slowly toward courtship. The Minotaur, though, still seemed ill at ease. He didn't like the impossible distances of the sky and the sea, and even the leafy greenery didn't make him feel safe the way a good labyrinth would have. In the end, the dwarves built him a small hut, a place much like his closet room on the *Basset*.

When they discovered several kinds of berries and fruit, the harpies were delighted with the island. They decided on a pie contest and asked the professor to be the judge, which caused him a rather tense afternoon. He could not, he knew, let one harpy be the winner (the screeching alone might kill him), and they were too smart to believe in a tie.

In the end he had a great inspiration and awarded the eldest a red ribbon for the tastiest crust, the second a little brass medallion for the best use of wild fruit and the youngest a silver pin for most unique shape.

Only Miranda could not be convinced to leave her endless dress-mending long enough to enjoy more than small pleasures. From time to time, she took out the little box Titania had given her. She wondered what was in it and yet could never quite bring herself to open it. Occasionally, she walked from the beach into the forest and brought back a flower, but most often her eyes were cast downward, as she snipped threads, mended seams and patched

Sewing seemed safe, simple and sensible to Miranda.

As the travelers rowed toward the island, the professor asked the mermaids who they might expect to find living there.

"Moths and moonflowers," said one.

"Blue-winged red birds," added another.

"Orange and yellow butterflies," yet another offered helpfully. For the remainder of the day, the travelers explored the expanse of beach and the nearby forest. As the mermaids had said, the only creatures were birds and butterflies. And though they made a brief sojourn on the isle and explored all but the crags, the travelers were quite alone.

The days passed lazily. Cassandra learned to swim nearly as well as the mermaids. Professor

torn places. Cassandra tried to distract her, but to no avail.

"Miranda, why don't you come into the water?"

"No," Miranda told her.

"Why not?" Cassandra demanded.

"I don't wish to," she said.

"You're just being an old stick," taunted Cassandra, hoping at least to make her sister angry. Miranda merely bent her head over her dress. While she sat and mended, she could keep her mother's memory close.

Cassandra saw swimming with a sea serpent as simply splendid.

Neither did Cassandra succeed in convincing her friend Sebastian to learn to swim, but since he would wade in the water searching for oysters and mussels, he was at least close enough to talk to. Cassandra told her father about the wonderful world under the water's surface. At first the professor wouldn't even go wading, but as Cassandra told him about the strange and wonderful things living in the mermaids' realm, his curiosity wouldn't let him rest.

"You should just see the little coral faeries, Daddy," Cassandra said.

"Coral faeries?" asked the professor. "What are they? Where did you see them?" He wrote in his journal about the creatures she had seen, but at last he had to see them himself. He took off his boots, rolled up his trousers and waded gingerly out to where the coral grew in brightly colored, mysterious formations. Journal in hand, he sat on a rock and peered into the water.

He was at last rewarded. A tiny form, colored gold and black like one of the bright fish, darted from the safety of one coral overhang to another. Then the professor discovered another one and another, each patterned like the fish with which they swam. He was so entranced that he failed to notice the incoming tide and ended up with thoroughly soaked trousers.

Coral faeries are related to, but harder to see than, these sisters of the sea.

Captain Malachi is concerned about the change in the professor's thinking.

The days passed blissfully. But one morning they all awakened with the feeling that it was time to go voyaging again. As they prepared to depart, the professor asked the mermaids if they would like to accompany the group on their travels.

"We are on an expedition, a most important voyage," said the professor. The mermaids laughed merrily and declined. The professor murmured to himself, "I don't suppose mermaids would add that much, but it would have been nice to show that sea serpent to someone. There's so much more to this than I thought. If people could just see these things, they'd believe."

Captain Malachi, standing behind the professor, stopped, concerned. "Who would he show the sea serpent to?" the captain wondered. He looked at Professor Aisling. But the professor wore a broad smile, and Captain Malachi let the matter go.

No one saw the professor try to convince one of the little coral faeries to swim into a bottle. The faeries hid in the coral and didn't come out again until the *Basset* sailed.

[68]

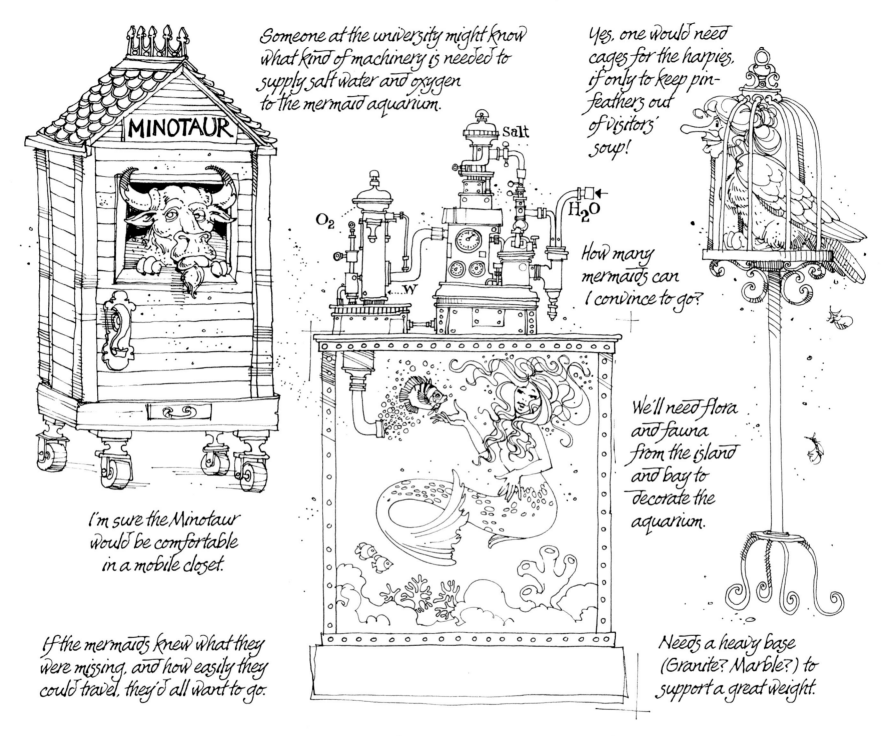

MINOTAUR

Someone at the university might know what kind of machinery is needed to supply salt water and oxygen to the mermaid aquarium.

Yes, one would need cages for the harpies, if only to keep pin-feathers out of visitors' soup!

O_2

W

salt

H_2O

How many mermaids can I convince to go?

I'm sure the Minotaur would be comfortable in a mobile closet.

We'll need flora and fauna from the island and bay to decorate the aquarium.

If the mermaids knew what they were missing, and how easily they could travel, they'd all want to go.

Needs a heavy base (Granite? Marble?) to support a great weight.

Some Thoughts on How to Display the Creatures

With just a little preparation, I could show my new friends the marvels of modern civilization. The containers are really for their comfort and safety. And imagine what scientists and London society would think of them!

They sailed for three days, and on the afternoon of the third they were startled to see several dark birds wheeling and gliding high above the ship. The air grew chill, as if they'd sailed into autumn, and the vultures appeared to be a bad omen. They made Cassandra shiver.

The captain looked through his spyglass for a long time. "My heart tells me that we must take great care here," he murmured. Only the professor seemed unaffected. He rubbed his hands together and said, "Now, Captain, let's not frighten everyone over a few old birds. Let us all go ashore. Who knows what marvels may be found?"

Even before they approached her, the Sphinx had glanced up at the vultures and faded silently below, presumably in search of riddle material. The harpies were right in the middle of kneading bread, and they had set the Minotaur to peeling carrots, potatoes and turnips to go into the soup they were planning to make.

The Manticore looked at his paws, saying he planned to sharpen his claws while it was quiet. He looked pointedly at the gremlins, who had not

only been very noisy that morning, but one of their number had tried using the Manticore's tail for a game of ringtoss. Still concerned, Captain Malachi went below and returned with a strange-looking gun, his ancient blunderbuss.

Despite the vultures, Cassandra was anxious to walk on dry land again. Miranda, however, declined.

"Miranda," asked her father, shaking his head, "what is all this? Aren't you being

a little silly? Besides, what could possibly happen?"

Accusing Miranda of being silly was enough. She thought the birds ugly and she didn't like the grim look on the captain's face, but she wouldn't be called silly for any reason. She climbed into the dinghy beside her sister.

The autumn colors of the island would have raised their spirits, except for the eerie feeling that they were being watched. Only the professor, searching avidly for new marvels, seemed untouched by nervousness or dread.

Only the professor seemed not to hear things creeping about in the undergrowth.

They discovered a stony track leading slowly up toward a dense woodland. As they pressed on, a pair of the gremlins stopped and looked at a footprint, sniffing and chattering in alarm. They pulled at Bosun Eli's sleeve and pointed it out to him. He in turn pulled the captain aside. Captain Malachi frowned but did not call out to the professor, who was already some distance ahead and shouting back at them to hurry. "Keep a sharp eye out," the captain told Eli and the gremlins.

They walked deeper into the woodland. Here, closed in by trees and brush, the feeling of gloom and hidden eyes watching grew far more intense. Cassandra shivered.

"Do you feel it?" she whispered to Miranda. "Don't you feel that we're being watched?"

"You're imagining things," Miranda said very quickly and began to hum a sprightly tune so that she wouldn't think about eyes in the forest. When a hawk screamed suddenly, she jumped and let out a little shriek. At that moment there was a sharp CRACK! from the forest. A broken tree limb splintered and fell, and with it came a figure, arms whirling madly. He crashed to the ground on his belly with a great "OOF!"

A tangled forest and the feeling of hidden eyes watching.

A brutish, unlovely fellow arose before the travelers. It is always difficult to be pretty when one has tusks, but this fellow's expression made him much the worse. He looked sneaky. He looked mean. And that is precisely what he was. Behind him the travelers could see four other figures, also clumsy and loutish and not terribly bright. They tripped and stepped on each other's feet.

"Trolls," growled Captain Malachi, renewing his grip on the blunderbuss.

Trolls! Smelly, dirty, clumsy, nasty, impolite . . . and those are their good points.

"Trolls?" said Professor Aisling in anticipation. "Excellent. Let us make their acquaintance. They seem a rather comic assemblage."

"Beware, Professor," Captain Malachi said softly.

"Of this lot?" the professor said with a derisive snort and a shake of his head. "Why, they're nothing more than an impromptu Punch and Judy show."

Swaggering and leering, the troll leader moved toward the travelers, and his motley band lumbered along behind. The troll chief walked right up to Cassandra. His eyes glittered as he stared at the little girl. He smiled a smile that was far, far worse than his frown.

"Good day to you all," said the professor. "I am Professor Algernon Aisling, leader of the *Basset* exploratory expedition—"

"Leader, eh?" asked the troll chieftain, never taking his eyes off Cassandra. "I am the great Skotos, fearless troll chief." He thumped his chest and looked directly at Cassandra, who shrank back against her father. Undeterred, Skotos leaned down and reached out a claw to touch her fair hair.

"Well, Leader of Whatever-it-was," he said, "you have some very lovely lasses here. Very nice."

"Er…well, er, thank you," said the professor, finally sensing a problem.

"Especially this little one with the golden-yellow hair," continued the leering troll. "Would you, would you like to sell her? I have gold, lots of gold. Gold for gold," he said, laughing at his little joke and touching Cassandra's fair hair once again.

"And what do you say to that, lass?" he asked

Trolls have become famous in literature for loitering under bridges waiting for goats.

They are natural followers, so a good or bad leader can determine their reputation for centuries.

TROLLS

Trolls are really only afraid of fire, though individually they are not quite as tough as they look.

Skotos admires young Cassandra.

Cassandra, putting his leering face close to hers and chucking her under the chin.

"Here, now!" The professor put himself between Skotos and Cassandra, and the troll chieftain found himself staring at the professor's waistcoat buttons. "I think you fellows had better be off about your own business," Professor Aisling said. Skotos stood up and looked him squarely in the eye.

"What, now? Can't have us a little jest now and again?" the troll asked in an aggrieved voice. The professor was unmoved by his protestations, and the dwarves moved toward the trolls.

"Think we don't have other things to do, more important business? Good-bye, leader," sneered Skotos. "For now," he muttered under his breath with a final leer at Cassandra. The trolls moved off down the trail in the direction the travelers had come. For some time the *Basset*'s passengers could hear the trolls' jeers and rude noises; then, finally, they were gone.

The travelers sighed with relief and continued their trek. Cassandra held her father's hand for *ten whole minutes* before she had to run ahead and pick up a sparkling rock. Then she walked back to show it to Sebastian. As the trail led into rocky hills, Sebastian began telling Cassandra the story of the Squintling Stone of Squingeburg.

When she got a small, sharp stone in her shoe, Cassandra plopped down on a rock and asked Sebastian to continue telling the story while she shook it out. Eli stayed behind with them as well. He had been to Squingeburg twice on holiday and had actually looked into the Squintling Stone. Soon Eli and Sebastian got into a small dispute over the rightful owner of the Squintling Stone. (This sort of preoccupation is always dangerous in troll country. But you'll hear of that soon enough.)

On the trail some distance ahead, and out of sight of Cassandra, the professor was thinking about cages. Ever since he had tried to capture, or at least coax, a coral faerie into a bottle, he had felt a little differently about the mythological creatures.

"Capturing a live coral faerie in the interest of scientific study isn't wrong, and that's all I wanted," he assured himself. "And trolls are quite nasty. I'm sure they *belong* in cages. But how to catch one?"

Just then, a terrified shriek brought him sharply back to the moment. He saw that Cassandra was missing. He and the others began to race back along the track, shouting her name. They found Eli and Sebastian lying on the ground, holding their heads but mostly unhurt. Cassandra was nowhere to be seen, but they heard a clatter of falling stones from the rocks above.

Eli and Sebastian have been attacked.

Something monstrous has grabbed Cassandra!

into the captain's hands just as the Gryphon gave a huge "SKRAWWWK!" and disappeared once more. The explorers ran pell-mell up the hill, leaping rocks and boulders to reach the top, where they saw the Gryphon again. Behind him, Cassandra pressed back against the cliff, screaming. Captain Malachi raised the blunderbuss to his shoulder and took aim, but Cassandra cried out, "No! No! Don't shoot *him!*" and she pointed to where Skotos and the troll band were rushing forward.

The crew confronts the creature.

"Where is she?!" the professor shouted, but before the injured dwarves could answer, they saw a fearsome sight. Rising above the rocks on powerful wings was a Gryphon— with Cassandra dangling below. It flew over a higher ledge of rocks and was gone!

The travelers scrambled up the rocks and had nearly reached the ledge when the Gryphon's head jumped forward at them, its beak gaping terrifyingly wide. "Shoot it, shoot it!" yelled the professor. In the confusion, however, the gremlins mistakenly loaded the old firearm with double the powder and none of the shot. They thrust the weapon

And only then did the travelers see the short troll spear protruding from the Gryphon's wing. The trolls, with much whooping and shouting, ran toward the wounded creature with clubs raised.

Again Cassandra screamed. Captain Malachi fell to one knee and aimed the old blunderbuss at the troll leader. As he fired, there was a huge BOOM! and a rush of smoke and flame.

Trolls again! . . . but firing the blunderbuss does the trick.

Flame exploded from the badly loaded gun, destroying its barrel and turning a standing deadwood into a crackling torch. As there was no shot, however, the trolls remained unharmed, but they were more afraid of fire than anything (except perhaps having their hair washed). They screamed, "FIRE! FIRE! RUN! GET AWAY!" and soon fled in a demoralized rout up into the rocks and boulders.

Attending to their new friend's wounds.

Well, as you can imagine, everyone (including the Gryphon) was quite ready to leave the troll island at once. Cassandra was shaking like a leaf, and Miranda would gladly have had dinner with a dozen harpies and sphinxes just to get away. While Sebastian bandaged the Gryphon's wounded wing as best he could, the professor apologized to the great beast for their having taken aim at him and then thanked him for helping Cassandra.

On the way back to the ship, the professor began to wonder again. After all, since the wuntarlabe had led them here, there must have been *something* for him to find. So, when they came back to the woodland and saw another path, the professor said, "This must be a shortcut to the beach," and he hurried down it before anyone could say yea or nay.

It was the smell they noticed first: a rank, moldy, cloying odor that grew more unpleasant as they went deeper into the wood. But it was the encampment they at last reached that caused them to stare,

[82]

aghast. The skulls of small animals adorned a dark doorway. Trees had been hacked into crude, horrifying carvings and made into roof supports for the lodge-house that was built into a shallow depression in an exposed hump of bedrock. Half-tanned skins were stretched out to dry on racks made of rib bones from some larger animal. Piles of rotting refuse lay off to one side, and when the wind stirred the foul air, the travelers gasped at the stench.

They were all in haste to be gone—all, that is, except the professor, who headed toward the dank lodge-house with a sleepwalker's drifting pace.

"Professor!" Captain Malachi called. "That's not a place for us. It's the trolls' lair."

Gryphon

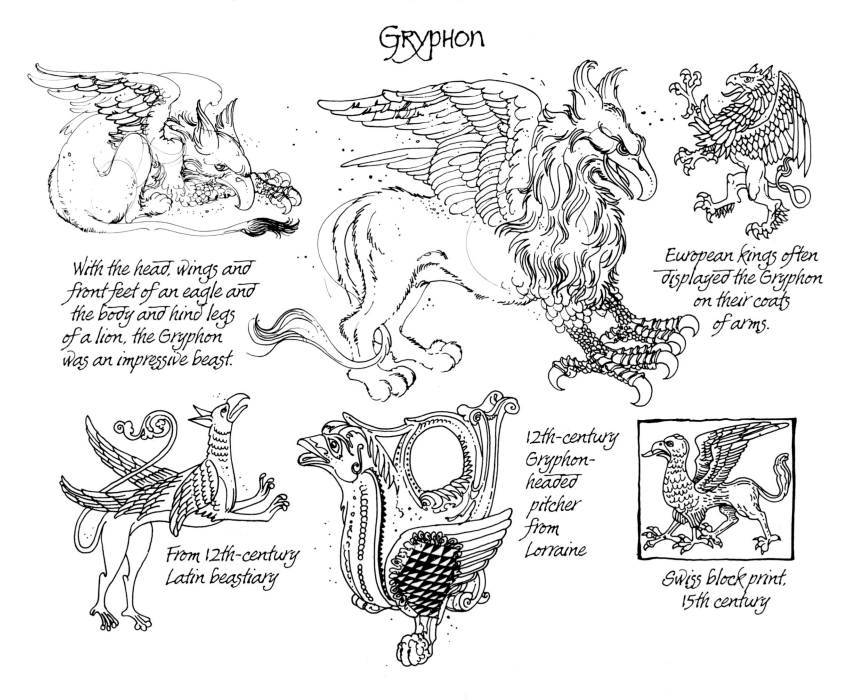

With the head, wings and front feet of an eagle and the body and hind legs of a lion, the Gryphon was an impressive beast.

European kings often displayed the Gryphon on their coats of arms.

From 12th-century Latin beastiary

12th-century Gryphon-headed pitcher from Lorraine

Swiss block print, 15th century

The lodge-house was dark, and at first Professor Aisling was unable to make out any details. But as his eyes adjusted to the gloom, he could see in the deepest recesses a slight glow given off by smoldering coals in a crude hearth. He started as a huge, dark bird squawked from its perch in the shadows, but still he went on. He crossed the floor, muttering, "It must be here. There must be something truly extraordinary."

He neared the fire pit, and in the flickering shadows cast upon the farther wall he saw what he had been seeking. Adorned with feathers and stones, it hung above a hewn slab of rock whereon lay other polished stones and bones and rattles decorated with woven grasses. The professor's footsteps echoed on the rough stone floor, and he felt a sudden chill rise between his shoulder blades. Weathered, ancient and huge, there was only one thing it could possibly be: a dragon skull.

The trolls' lair smelled as bad as it looked.

"Professor," asked Sebastian with some alarm, "what have you got there?"

"A dragon skull!" he said. "Do you know, do you have any idea, what this means? *There were dragons*! This is more than I could ever have hoped to find! Come on," he urged, fearful of being caught when the trolls returned. "Let's be off to the *Basset*!"

"Then you'd best put it back," Sebastian stated.

"What?!" the professor cried, clutching the skull to his chest.

"Professor Aisling, we don't want some foulness from a troll lair on the ship."

The professor decided to take the trolls' most prized possession.

"It's a dragon skull, nothing to do with trolls."

"And those baubles swinging from it, aren't they such decoration as trolls would use?" asked Sebastian. The professor ripped them away.

"What baubles?" he asked. Cassandra tugged at her father's sleeve.

"But, Daddy, we can't take that," she said matter-of-factly.

"Whyever not?" he asked, exasperated now.

"Because it isn't ours—"

"Cassandra, I know that you don't understand, but this is my proof. Proof," he repeated.

"But, Daddy, it's stealing," she said. The professor sighed in frustration.

"Cassandra, the trolls obviously came by this in some horrid way, so what I'm doing isn't really stealing." He looked down at her, adding, "You're just a little child, and of course you cannot see how the grown-up world really works. Now come along, everyone." And he turned and hurried down the path toward the shore.

Cassandra stood unmoving. Beneath her gown, Titania's stone had grown as cold as ice. She took it into her hand, but even though she held it tight, it did not warm up in her palm. The tiny, comforting pulse that she had come to expect upon holding the stone was stilled. She shuddered suddenly, knowing absolutely that the silent cold was a warning.

"Daddy, this is wrong!" she cried as if in pain.

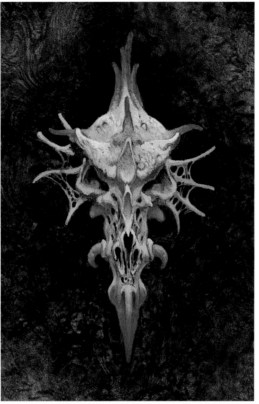

Seeing this proof, Bilgewallow would have to eat his words.

"Put it back or something bad will happen!" But Professor Aisling was already far ahead on the trail, still clutching the dragon skull to his chest as though it were made of gold. The other travelers drew close to Cassandra, whose face was white above her hands clenching Titania's stone. For a few moments Miranda took her sister's hands in her own. Then, heeding Sebastian's insistence, Miranda gently, but still with haste, urged Cassandra forward. Soon everyone was hurrying toward the beach and looking over their shoulders for signs of trolls.

They had just reached the beach and clambered into the dinghy when they heard a horrific howling from the forest. They began to row frantically toward the *Basset*. Fortunately, they were already some distance into deep water when the trolls poured onto the beach, still howling their rage like a pack of maddened dogs.

Skotos ran right to the edge of the water (though not into it, for trolls hate bathing). He shook his fists and jumped up and down in wrath and frustration. "After them!" he yowled. "AFTER THEM!"

"But, but we don't have a boat!" bawled his lieutenant, Mog. Skotos wheeled on him as if he might gnash him with his teeth. Instead he settled for shoving the cringing Mog, who yelped and fell with a splash into the surf.

"Then find one, you fool," snarled Skotos.

rofessor Aisling seemed not to be the same person. He sat at a small table on deck but took no notice of his surroundings at all. If asked, he said he was studying the skull. He had beside him a magnifying glass, measuring tape and calipers, but he did not seem to use them. He just held the skull in his hands and stared dreamily at it. When anyone spoke to him, the professor looked blankly at the speaker, like someone newly awakened from a deep sleep.

Cassandra was frightened. Her father no longer teased her or made playful conversation. He didn't even notice that she had discarded her own tattered dress and now wore borrowed dwarf-clothing.

Added to this was the constant nervous activity of the dwarves. They more often looked behind than ahead, obviously worried that the trolls might have followed them. This made both girls even more anxious and they, too, often scanned the horizon for troll pursuers. The other passengers seemed to draw into themselves. Where once they had all gathered in the galley for meals, the passengers now picked at this or that or even skipped meals altogether. The harpies all but stopped cooking. Finding their newly discovered cooking talents unappreciated, they became depressed. It was a rather ill-tempered depression, noisily punctuated by their birdlike exclamations, but a depression nonetheless. Still, it made no difference whether they shrieked or were quiet. No one had the heart to care about food.

Yet when they reached landfall again, the professor at last looked up from the dragon skull and scanned the approaching shoreline with obvious interest. Cassandra was at first relieved. But all was not well. She saw him carry the skull into his chamber, and when he came out he took great care to lock the door, something he had never done before. She grew even more worried.

When she told Miranda about it, her sister told her not to worry. But Cassandra saw her older sister bite her lip as she looked at their father, so she was neither fooled nor greatly comforted.

The tiny island they rowed toward was a wooded and rocky promontory rising from the waves, with a white stone building near the summit. "Who knows what fine specimens we'll find here?" the professor asked. Captain Malachi looked at him, surprised and in some alarm.

"'Specimens'?" he repeated back to the professor, as though he might not have heard correctly.

"But of course, old man! Yes! This voyage could make my reputation, don't you know," he said jovially. Everyone nearby, Cassandra included, stood with their mouths open, but the professor never noticed a bit of it. He was looking forward to the new shore and thinking about how he could make Bilgewallow eat his words.

Everyone hoped exploring a new isle would make the professor forget the dragon skull.

Once ashore, they wandered in and out of groves and woodlands for some time without seeing anything or anyone. The professor appeared to be getting impatient as nothing extraordinary presented itself. Finally, they entered a pretty little grove, and he glumly suggested that they have lunch.

"Please take care not to trample the flowers or pull the vines," a nearby tree said in a soft voice.

"Excuse me," said Professor Aisling to the tree, "but did you speak?"

"I did," replied the tree.

"Amazing," the professor said to himself. "What manner of tree are you that you can speak?" he asked.

"I am not a tree," the tree replied.

"Then what manner of being are you?" asked the professor, perplexed.

Above them the leaves began to rustle, and they watched as branches parted to reveal an innocent, feminine face. She smiled shyly out at them.

"A dryad," the professor said softly. Then he murmured to himself, "Just wait till Bilgewallow sees this!" Then to the dryad, "Fair lady of the tree, you are indeed as lovely as I was given to believe. In fact, more so."

[90]

The dryad, unused to flattery, blushed. "Which is why it would be a sad loss if a being such as yourself were to fade from existence," continued the professor. The dryad looked alarmed. "But fortunately, Oberon, King of the Faeries, has charged me, his humble emissary, with your safety and transport." The dryad's life among the leaves left her naive in the ways of deception. But Cassandra and Miranda (and all the other travelers) were shocked. Cassandra reached out a hand and tugged on the professor's coat.

"Daddy," she said, "that's not—"

"Hush!" he hissed. "Children should be seen and not heard." Cassandra was shocked into silence, but the professor didn't notice the hurt look on her face. He was intent on convincing the dryad that both she and her tree could be accommodated on the *Basset*.

"Professor," Captain Malachi broke in, "I don't know that we *can* take care of a dryad and her tree. You know a dryad cannot leave her tree, and a tree needs an awful lot of water—"

"Then we'll just fill more barrels," said the professor with a shrug.

"But, sir, we cannot be responsible for the health of the dryad's tree. If the tree dies, then she dies."

"Captain Malachi, thank you for your concern. But if the dryad is willing to go, I don't think it need trouble you any further."

NEREID

OREID

DRYAD

Like nereids from the ocean and oreids from caves and grottoes, dryads are nymphs. Dryads inhabit trees and cannot live if their tree is killed.

So without more ado, they dug up the dryad's tree and headed back to the ship. They had gone much of the way back when the professor noticed a narrow trail passing under an old willow. He insisted that they follow it, and it led them to an old garden. What claimed their attention immediately was the astonishingly lifelike statuary scattered through-out. Everyone gathered around the sculptures, amazed at their realism. Professor Aisling walked over to where a stone squirrel sat atop a stone owl. He leaned down and peered at the stone.

"How odd," he said, turning to the others. "The owl looks a great deal older than the squirrel, as if some sculptor had returned a hundred years after creating the first and said, 'I think I'll just add a lit-tle something up here.'" Another statue, an old stone monk with a book in his hand, was particu-larly compelling. "I've seen a great deal of sculp-ture over the years," said the professor, "but never have I seen anything so perfectly lifelike."

"And with good reason," said a dry and rather arrogant voice from somewhere off in the over-grown shrubbery.

"Are you another dryad?" asked the professor, scanning the leaves for sight of the speaker.

"How insulting!" said the invisible speaker with undisguised hauteur. "I am *not* a dryad. Must I spend a thousand years in exile only to be insulted at the end of it?"

"I most humbly beg your pardon, madam. But will you not show yourself, at least?" asked the professor.

[92]

"No indeed," answered the voice, "unless you are all as blind as bats. You will notice, I hope, that there are no bats, nor moles either for that matter, in my garden. No, if you would make conversation with me, you must keep your eyes closed or your face turned away from me at all times. This you must obey or find yourself at gravest peril. And," the voice continued imperiously, "there are far too many of you. Send those silly small creatures off. I cannot be responsible for their antics."

In sudden understanding, the professor excitedly herded everyone out of the garden without so much as a by-your-leave. "Could it be she?" the professor asked himself with a flutter of anticipation. He prepared to be horrified. Captain Malachi growled that he was unused to being referred to as a silly small creature.

From the secretive greenery of a lovely old garden came a mysterious voice.

"Come, come, Captain," said the professor. "I'm sure she didn't mean anything by her words. Does anyone have a bit of mirror?" The gremlins began to search through their hats, but Miranda quickly pulled a small hand mirror from one of her pockets. Without even saying thank you, the professor took it and hurried back into the garden.

"You do," she said. Then the travelers heard nothing for several moments.

"What's he doing?" asked Miranda. They could only listen and therefore couldn't know that when Medusa stepped into the garden, the professor had looked into the mirror and discovered that, despite having a great many live snakes instead of hair,

Medusa

Greek beauty cursed with the power to turn those who look into her eyes to stone. She and her two unattractive sisters were known as the Gorgons. The snakes were also part of the gods' punishment.

Cassandra and Miranda looked at each other, shaking their heads. Whatever had come over their father, they didn't like it at all. But there was nothing to be done about it for the moment. Instead, the travelers drew close to the hedge. If they couldn't come in, they could at least listen.

"Do I have the honor of addressing the fabled Medusa?" they heard the professor ask.

Medusa was incredibly, undeniably beautiful.

"I am delighted to make your acquaintance, milady," Professor Aisling said finally.

"Yes, I suppose it isn't just everyday that one engages a monster in conversation."

"I don't believe you are a monster, milady," said the professor gently.

"Why not?" she replied bitterly. "When my only

companions are those I've turned to cold stone."

The thought struck Professor Aisling that such must be a very bitter reminder indeed, and in the face of it he had no wise words to offer. Instead he began to tell her of the voyage and of his errand.

"I am aware of your voyage, Professor, and I should like to accompany you.

I've grown so very tired of being eternally alone." Although she stood calmly, perhaps even haughtily, around her head the snakes writhed into tortuous forms, hissing madly.

"But of course, dear lady. Of course you shall accompany us, though I hope one day to know *how* everyone knows of our voyage."

Captain Malachi was much less enthusiastic. He had sent dwarves and gremlins on ahead with the dryad to make sure that her tree didn't dry out, but the captain was not prepared to have a Gorgon aboard.

"Professor, I don't see how we can run a ship while risking that one of us be turned to stone for rounding the wrong corner."

"Come now, old man, aren't you overstating the case just a bit? We'll get her settled on the ship in some nice, cozy place, and then I'm sure that everybody will just work around Medusa without any fuss at all."

"Professor, I must object. We're going to have quite the time seeing to the dryad, but Medusa is just too dangerous. Why, sir, one of your own daughters might run afoul of those eyes—not that the lady would be so cruel, but that she can't help how her gaze works."

"Captain Malachi, this is my expedition, and I am quite certain that this is the proper course of action. I don't see that there need be any further discussion on the subject."

A shocked Captain Malachi stepped back as though he had been struck. Cassandra almost cried out at her father. She hated for anyone to be cruel, and she was suddenly afraid to speak to him. He was so changed. It was as if he were not even the same person.

Thus, it was a subdued and not very happy group who returned to the shore. Medusa followed at a safe distance. Sensibly, no one looked back. The trouble with having a Gorgon aboard began at the shore. While

Eli bravely helped Medusa aboard.

everyone was rowed back to the *Basset*, Medusa sat with her back to the water and waited for Eli to return. Eli, with his back to the Gorgon, called out that it was time for her to climb into the boat. She then had to climb in unassisted, and turn so her back was safely to Eli, who then turned toward Medusa's back so he could row them back to the *Basset*.

Medusa was also required to climb up to the ship without assistance, though at the rail Eli, wearing a kerchief over his eyes, kindly reached down a

hand to help her onto the deck. From that moment on, nothing could be done simply.

Once back on the ship, the professor seemed to forget the dryad and Medusa entirely. He went back to "examining" the dragon skull. He ignored the uproar around him. Knowing that he would be of no help, none of the crew approached him any longer. All duties aboard the ship were slowed to a snail's pace. As if in sympathy to their plight, even the wuntarlabe worked slowly, sluggishly.

It's really hard to work around a Gorgon!

Disasters happen regularly wherever Medusa goes. The harpies, never very patient, screech over ruined recipes—and so all suffer.

Everything is backward!

Gremlins just can't seem to avoid mischief. One day they tried to tease Medusa's snakes.

While Medusa is on deck, chores must be done (or, more often, NOT done) backward.

After the first few days the crew tried to convince Medusa to stay below, but she refused. "I did not come aboard to spend my time alone," she said.

At last, they managed to persuade her to spend part of each day in her quarters. During those few hours, the ship's work went back to normal. But when the Gorgon came up to take the air, everyone else was forced to work blindfolded or by carrying hand mirrors and walking backward.

The gremlins weren't good at this. Medusa tried very diligently to avoid them for their own sakes, but after only a few days at sea, there had been several near misses. Even the harpies had gotten confused enough to mix anchovies into their pancake batter and put salt in the tea.

None of this did Professor Aisling notice. He sat at his table on deck, writing in his journal or stroking the dragon skull. On the day that a luckless gremlin went overboard, he didn't hear the great splash and all the shouting that went up around him, or even realize that the *Basset* had come to a halt.

The unwary gremlin had been in the wrong place at the wrong time. While trying to steal a sweet from the galley, he'd nearly come face to face with Medusa. In his panic, the unfortunate gremlin had bumbled, stumbled and tumbled overboard.

THE GREAT DISCOVERER

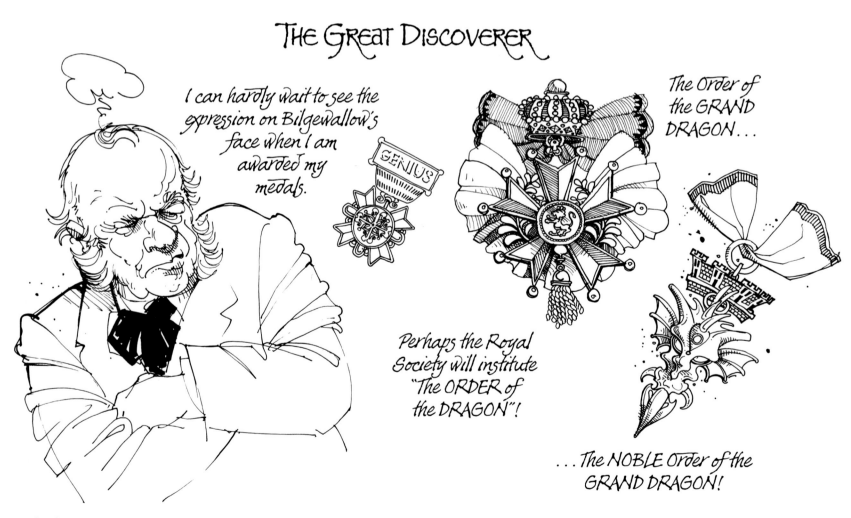

I can hardly wait to see the expression on Bilgewallow's face when I am awarded my medals.

GENIUS

The Order of the GRAND DRAGON . . .

Perhaps the Royal Society will institute "The ORDER of the DRAGON"!

. . . The NOBLE Order of the GRAND DRAGON!

Quickly, Medusa raised the alarm with a shout. She stared straight up so that anyone hearing her and running to help would not be turned to stone. As the dwarves, gremlins and Cassandra ran to the side of the boat, a stone gull crashed at Medusa's feet. "Drat," she said. "There are days when it does not pay to rise at all." She sat in a corner with her eyes closed while the crew fished their sodden companion from the water.

Once the captain had made certain that nothing worse than a dunking had befallen the gremlin, he walked across the deck to the professor, who did not look up when Malachi approached.

Miranda is concerned for her father.

I must write my acceptance speech for the reception at the Royal College.

Esteemed gentlemen of the College
I am most humbly grateful
no, no that won't do
mustn't grovel.
they won't respect that

Gentlemen of the College
LOOK before you
no, too Brusque.
I must have just the right attitude

Esteemed colleagues, I have invited
a
you here today to share with
the world my most extraordinary
discoveries...
(wait for applause)

"Professor Aisling," said the captain tersely, "a word with you, sir."

The professor looked up in annoyance. "Yes, what is it?" he asked.

"Are you aware, sir, that one of the crew members has fallen overboard and had to be rescued?"

"Well, as you've already rescued him, whatever do you want to interrupt me about it for?"

"Professor Aisling, the *Basset*'s motto is, in fact, 'By believing, one sees,'" said the captain.

"Thank you for your excellent translation," said the professor sarcastically.

"I think, Professor, that you have lost your way," the captain replied. He turned on his heel and strode toward the wheelhouse.

"What nonsense!" Professor Aisling scoffed after him. Cassandra, who had crept close to her father's side, looked up sadly at his face.

"He's right, Daddy," she said quietly. The professor slammed down his pen and stood up, kicking back his chair.

"It is obvious that I have been far too lax in my discipline. From now on, Cassandra, you will speak only when spoken to."

"But, Daddy—" The professor rounded on her as if he might strike her.

"DID YOU HEAR ME? I SAID, *BE SILENT*!"

Several horrifyingly disastrous things occurred at once. Medusa, startled by the shout, whirled toward it and dropped her teacup, which shattered on the deck. Cassandra spun toward the sound, and Sebastian, seeing Cassandra and Medusa on a visual collision course, flung himself between them.

There was a loud CRACK! and a bright flash, as if lightning had struck the *Basset*. Where Sebastian had leapt up, a stone statue fell to the deck. Aghast, Medusa clapped her hands over her eyes. Cassandra screamed and ran

[100]

to the statue. Feeling cold, hard stone beneath her hands, she shrieked and began to weep. Turning to her father, she cried out, "This is all your fault! I HATE YOU!"

In horror, Professor Aisling looked around at the stricken faces of his companions. No one would meet his eyes. The dwarves went to kneel near Cassandra, who lay weeping where Sebastian had fallen. The shocked gremlins huddled silently

together. "I didn't mean for this to happen!" he cried. "Captain, surely you know that I—" But Captain Malachi didn't look at him. He, too, knelt beside Sebastian.

Horrified, the professor turned to his table and the dragon skull. With a cry, he picked up the skull and threw it away from him. It hit the deck and bounced away toward the water. Then he fled the deck in despair.

Tragedy befalls the expedition.

assandra lay sobbing on the deck beside Sebastian until she felt someone gently take her hand and pull her away. She turned to see her sister. Miranda pulled Cassandra into her arms. Still sobbing, Cassandra cried out, "Oh, Miranda! He's dead! Sebastian's *dead*!"

Lying there, Sebastian truly did seem to be dead. Captain Malachi and the other dwarves stood him upright, but they couldn't balance him, for he had been leaping when he had met Medusa's gaze. Instead of laying him back down, they lashed him to a mast. With Sebastian once more in a standing position, it seemed as if they might one day have their friend back again.

When nothing more could be done for Sebastian, everyone suddenly realized that the *Basset* had stopped. Her sails were raised and a fair breeze blew, but the little ship did not respond. Captain Malachi called for Archimedes and one of the gremlins to work the wuntarlabe. And then they discovered that the situation was even worse. The workings of the wuntarlabe were frozen in place. Archimedes could not set it, nor could any of the gremlins spin the wheel.

The professor, who had locked himself away since the mishap, would not respond to knocks on his door. The concerned captain called the crew and passengers together and gravely said, "Ladies and gentlemen, I'm afraid that we are becalmed." For some minutes there was a bit of uproar while everyone cried, "What? What? Becalmed? How can that be?" But there was no getting away from it. The *Basset* wouldn't move.

"Harrumph!" snorted the Manticore. "Though the Gryphon's wing isn't yet mended enough to carry him far, I could fly east and the Sphinx west to see—" But Captain Malachi quietly interrupted.

"That is a generous offer," said the captain, "but, as you know, the *Basset* is no ordinary ship. It was the professor's belief that powered this vessel. It was his belief that brought us all together. We are all needed here and we are all needed together. What we must do is discover how to help the professor find his way. We must each do what we can, but together."

Well, the harpies looked at each other and said, "Soup!"—which was their answer to every trouble in the world. Cassandra was far too sad to do anything but sit by Sebastian and hold tight to Titania's stone. The little stone was warm once more and pulsed steadily in her hand, but it couldn't lift her downcast heart. Miranda sat down by Cassandra. Without saying anything, she snuggled close to her sister and wrapped her arms around the little girl. She rocked gently and hummed a song their mother had often sung to them. Cassandra's eyelids fluttered and soon she was fast asleep.

Bosun Eli had an idea. He didn't know if it would help the professor find his way, but he thought it might make someone feel better. He went to the galley where the harpies had begun cooking. He took a bit of soup, a cup of tea and several sugar biscuits, put

Cassandra wouldn't leave Sebastian's side.

them on a small tray and took it to Medusa. When he reached the door, he tied his kerchief over his eyes and knocked. "Who is it?" she asked, sounding ill at ease. "Bosun Eli, ma'am," he replied. "I've brought a tray." Medusa guided him in and asked about the rest of the travelers. He told her that the professor had locked himself in his chamber and would neither open the door nor speak to anyone. When Eli told her that the captain had said they must stay together to find a solution, she gave a deep sigh of relief. "I was afraid everyone might wish me to be gone," she said. "No," said Eli. "You are part of our journey now."

Captain Malachi paced the deck and turned to look where Archimedes stood. Their helmsman seemed at a loss, as if having no employment at the wheel left him adrift. Some distance away, Augustus, too, stood uncomfortably idle. When the seaman looked his way, Captain Malachi waved him over.

"I think it would be wise," he said, addressing both Archimedes and Augustus, "to post a watch fore and aft."

"Trolls," nodded Augustus in comprehension.

"Yes," replied the captain. "The longer we lie becalmed, the greater our danger. I'd like the two of you to take the first watch with a couple of gremlins. We cannot ask them to stay on guard by themselves, I'm afraid. Though they've got the sharpest eyes aboard, they aren't capable of being still long enough to watch alone. Eli and I will take second watch. It would be best if we had three changes at the watch, but we shall make do with two."

At the captain's order, Archimedes had brightened immediately. The *Basset*'s helmsman was a calm, steady worker, fearless even in rough seas and all but tireless, but inactivity weighed upon him. At least having a watch and gremlins to mind would keep him from feeling like a boat off its moorings. Augustus nodded thoughtfully and stroked his luxuriant mustache.

"What about the Sphinx and the Manticore, Captain?" he asked. "They might be willing to take a watch as well, sir."

"An excellent idea, Augustus. I'll ask them myself. Where is Bosun Eli?"

"Gone below to take a tray to the Gorgon," said Augustus, with a look of distaste.

"We're all worried about Sebastian, Augustus, but we cannot lay the blame for what happened at her door," the captain said kindly but firmly.

IN THE DOLDRUMS

The magic that had powered the Basset—and the expedition—was gone. The banner that had flown so merrily above now lay slack against its standard. At times breezes blew, but still the banner lay unmoving and the little ship refused the call. The ship's motto, Credendo vides, was all but forgotten.

An air of gloom overtook the travelers. The Sphinx no longer searched for a riddle. The Manticore stopped watching over the expedition. The harpies made soup, but though they fussed over the recipe, the travelers were too despondent and anxious to take comfort from the meal.

The gremlins, who were usually so irrepressible and ready for any kind of mischief, sat huddled together. Subdued and listless, they declined even to brush their hats.

Only Eli seemed from the first to have a purpose. He had always felt sorry for Medusa's loneliness, but as the days passed and he brought tea and biscuits, there grew between them a deep friendship.

[105]

After Eli left, Medusa paced her chamber. "That fool of a professor should be out trying to find a solution rather than moping in his room," she told herself. "It was his fault." Her snakes hissed. She paced up and down her room some more. Finally she decided that if no one else could get his attention, she would give him a talking-to he wouldn't soon forget.

She found his chamber door open and the room empty. "Well, where has he got to?" she asked herself. Passing the great double doors of the library, she heard a muffled voice and the thump of great books being dropped on a table. She called out to him.

"Yes?" he asked in a weary voice.

"Professor, why have you locked yourself in the library when the ship goes nowhere?"

"Milady," he answered her through the door, "truly I cannot stop for conversation. Somewhere in this vast collection of science and research there must be an answer on how to reverse Sebastian's problem. There must be some way I can undo what I have caused…I must keep looking," he said as she heard his footsteps recede.

"Wait!" she cried. The footsteps stopped. "I'll help you," she said.

"Why?"

"Because…," she paused as she thought about the answer herself. "Because there is nothing else I *can* do. I cannot go above, not now, and yet I cannot bear to be alone." She heard the snick of the lock being opened. She waited until she was sure he had walked safely away, and then she slipped inside.

Medusa approached a despairing Professor Aisling.

When Bosun Eli next brought a tray to Medusa's door, he discovered her gone. The dwarf went searching for her (though very carefully and using a pocket mirror). Hearing the low murmur of conversation from the library, he smiled. He recalled an old dwarf saying: *First heal the spirit; then right what's wrong.* The harpies, Eli told himself, would add something right in the middle: *feed the body,* which was also a good idea. Eli went to fetch another tray.

So it went for days. The professor, aided by Medusa, searched for an answer. Eli brought them trays of food. But at last the professor knew that the answer had eluded him. In an orderly way, he had looked up every single collection, qualification, inspection and experimentation he could find. Indeed, he had read *anything* that might help with Sebastian. Finding nothing, he sank into despair.

Sitting several shelves away, Medusa became aware that it had been a long time since she had heard anything from the professor. Carefully, she went looking for him. She found him bent low over the table, head in hands. She saw him shudder and realized that he was weeping. She walked quietly away and then called out.

"Professor?" She heard him clear his throat. "Yes?"

"Have we failed to discover the answer you sought? Have we perhaps been searching in the wrong place?"

"No," he answered. "*I* have failed." The utter despair in his voice touched her heart, but she had no answer for him. For she, too, in all the long years of her curse, had found no solution for reversing what was done.

On the fourth day, at precisely three o'clock in the afternoon, many things happened at once. The captain called Eli, Augustus and Archimedes into his cabin for a meeting. There he made a suggestion that caused the other dwarves to gasp. "I think," he said, "that it may be our only option. If we linger, the trolls will surely find us."

"But, sir!" Augustus whispered tensely. "No mortal has ever been taken there!" At that moment Miranda rapped on the door.

"I know," replied the captain, opening the door, "but it may be the only place the professor will be able to find the answer." Malachi looked at Miranda. "I think the College is where we must go."

Miranda didn't speak or even wait to hear more. "A college!" she thought. "That sounds so…so *sensible*." She fairly flew to where Cassandra sat.

"Cassandra!" Miranda cried breathlessly. "Captain Malachi says that there's a college where they'll be able to help Sebastian."

For the first time since the tragedy, Cassandra showed a ray of hope. Pausing only long enough

The captain and crew were terribly concerned when the Wuntarlabe wouldn't work.

to give her little sister a quick hug, Miranda went to the library and knocked.

"Father?" she called through the door. "Father, Captain Malachi says there's a place that can help Sebastian. It's some college they know of." Hope leapt in his heart, then as quickly died. "What greater science could they offer?" he asked himself.

Back in his cabin, Captain Malachi rubbed his chin. There was still the problem of the wuntarlabe.

"I wish I could talk to Oberon," he said to Eli. "He would know what to do." Behind him, a bell chimed. He whirled around to see the wuntarlabe sparkling and vibrating. The dwarves gasped. This sort of thing had never, ever happened before. Untouched, unset, the wuntarlabe had come to life. They heard the loud PING! and then two THWOCKS! and a CLICK! Then the great bejeweled pointer swung round and round and round. With a decisive SNICK! it pointed THAT WAY!

which just happened to be toward the College of Magical Knowledge. The *Basset*'s sails filled with wind, and the little ship began to move.

"Well, I guess that's the answer," Malachi said.

Medusa and the professor both felt the sudden tug of wind on the *Basset*. He was wondering how to take his leave of her without being impolite when she said, "I think, Professor, that it's time for you to go above."

That wasn't quite what troubled Professor Aisling, though. He found, now that there was reason to leave the library, that he would miss Medusa—snakes, lethal gaze and all.

"Milady," suggested the professor, "perhaps you could come above as well, if I—"

"No, Professor Aisling. Although it was an accident, I have helped you cause enough grief. I shall stay below. Our good bosun keeps me supplied with tea and news."

The professor stood a moment, undecided. He was reluctant to leave Medusa alone but was also anxious to go above.

"Ah, here you are then, Professor Aisling," said Malachi as the professor joined him. "Miss Miranda has told you of our destination?" the captain asked as the professor walked uncertainly to his side.

"The College? Yes. But I have been searching through all the most recently published journals, books and treatises—"

Captain Malachi interrupted him. "I would say, Professor, that science offers only one way to look at our problem," the captain said mildly. "And we make not for a college such as you might know. We sail toward the College of Magical Knowledge."

Standing next to her father, Miranda was disappointed with the College's name. "I should have known it wouldn't be anything sensible," she thought, "but fortunately we're moving."

Fortunate indeed! Also precisely at three o'clock, the trolls got their vessel afloat. Not that it mattered to them what time it was, for they didn't wear pocket watches. What did matter was that Skotos had gotten his boat. It was an odd vessel, found derelict and outfitted through slapdashery. Mog, who had found the boat, was given a silver piece when Skotos discovered some fine, though strange, armor and weapons in one of the holds.

Mog was still Skotos' second in command, but the other three lodge-house members—Fracas, Gourdo and Bob (short, of course, not for Robert but for Bobalogogtwit)—had been promised new titles if they could convince their cousins to join the Great Troll Revenge Expedition. Fracas and Gourdo had each enlisted five of their cousins, but Bob, who had always been the least popular of them (he didn't scowl often enough), outdid himself by persuading thirteen of his cousins to come along.

Skotos smiled a very nasty smile as they sailed out of the bay. When none of the others was near, he pulled from a hiding place a small patch of blue cloth and a single pale golden hair. Professor Thief would pay the price of robbing Skotos, the Great Troll Leader. He would get his dragon skull back, and the little Gold-hair, too.

The trolls prepared to hunt down the professor.

assandra didn't quite dare to hope. She certainly didn't dare to speak to her father. She had told him she hated him, and that weighed like a stone upon her heart. Fortunately for her peace of mind, the passage to the College of Magical Knowledge wasn't of long duration.

Since the gentlemen of the College were unused to the company of strangers—to say nothing of mortals visiting unannounced—only Cassandra, Miranda and Professor Aisling accompanied the dwarves. "That will be quite enough for me to explain," said Captain Malachi.

The path to the College led upward into the mountains. Augustus and Archimedes, the youngest and strongest, carried Sebastian between them, lashed to a stout pole. When they reached the gates of the College, Captain Malachi stepped up to the heavy plank door and knocked loudly.

Cassandra heard slow, shuffling steps. The footsteps neared the door. A small panel in the door slid open. She saw a nose. Breathing wheezily, the nose's owner said,

"Who's there?"

"Captain Malachi of the *Basset*, sir."

"Young," *wheeze*, "Malachi!" *huff*. "Who's that with you," *huff*, "lad?"

"Professor Algernon Aisling and his daughters, Miranda and Cassandra."

"Mortals!" *wheeze*. "But why have you brought them here?"

"Our first mate, Sebastian, has been turned to stone in an encounter with Medusa. We want to find a way to restore him to his former self."

"But," *wheeze*, "mortals, young Malachi?"

"It was the wuntar-labe that directed

us here," Captain Malachi answered confidently.

"Well," *huff*, "you'd best," *wheeze*, "come in then."

Cassandra never forgot her first sight of the College of Magical Knowledge. The corridors were quite as corridors should be, but the gentlemen moving to and fro were extraordinary. They didn't look like gentlemen from the university where her father worked. In London, a learnèd gentleman wore black and was very serious. Not at the College of Magical Knowledge. These gentlemen wore as many colors as one could imagine, plus two. "Learning must be a great deal more fun here," she whispered to Miranda.

The wonderful College of Magical Knowledge.

Oddly, these well-dressed gentlemen, after getting over the surprise of finding mortals in their midst, looked pityingly upon and laughed at the clothes Captain Malachi and the other dwarves wore. Finally, the Oldest Professor said to the dwarves, "Off you go, lads. I'll take your friends in to supper and meet you there."

"But where are they all going?" Cassandra asked the Oldest Professor, who reminded her of Sebastian, only gruffer.

"Eh? Well, you can't expect them," *wheeze*, "to meet their colleagues dressed like *that*. The *Basset* crew are very important individuals. They need to put on the garments their positions require." While they were sitting down to a cold supper, Malachi and the others returned, dressed in colorful finery. The professor noticed that he wasn't offered any new clothes.

"Now that we are all," *wheeze*, "prepared, perhaps we can discover what it is," *huff*, "that you need to learn," said the Oldest Professor.

"I'm not here to learn," said Professor Aisling. "I just want to get an answer to our problem."

"An answer?" asked the Oldest Professor. "Well, if that's all you need," *huff*, "I suppose," *wheeze*, "you *could* consult the Book of Answers—" The dwarves gave a collective groan of protest.

"But that's it!" cried Professor Aisling. "We need answers. We don't have time to waste on foolishness!"

The gentlemen of the College knew how to dress for success.

[114]

Augustus and Eli, elegantly attired.

Cassandra thought that the Learnèd Custodian of the Answers looked as if he thought very well of himself. He stood above them, holding a very small book. The Learnèd Custodian of the Answers, however, was impressive enough in both dress and demeanor to make up for the smallness of his text.

"First querent," he said in a voice that sounded as if it had had to travel through marbles.

"How do we change a dwarf back from stone?" asked the professor.

"'Dwarf,'" read the Learnèd Custodian. "'Being of small stature with enormous capacity for serious occupation.' Subheadings: 'busy dwarves, fat dwarves, happy dwarves, idle dwarves, inebriated dwarves, sad dwarves, thin dwarves, wayward dwarves, worried dwarves.' Hmm. 'Dwarf sun'. . . there is no subheading for stone dwarves," said the Learnèd Custodian of the Answers, "therefore, there are no stone dwarves."

"Well, actually, he was *turned* to stone—"

The Custodian silenced the professor with a look.

"'Stone: building stone, cornerstone, curbstone, paving stone, turnstone,' no, that won't do; it's a bird. 'Stone: common dense minerals, fieldstone, flint, granite, lodestone, marble, shale, slate—'"

"This isn't quite what we—" Again the Custodian silenced the professor with a haughty glance.

"'Stone,'" continued the Learnèd Custodian, "'See also: rock, boulder, pebble.'" The Learnèd Custodian of the Answers looked down his nose at Sebastian. "Well, he's hardly a pebble, is he?" The dwarves were all rubbing their temples as if they had suddenly gotten headaches.

"Perhaps we have worded the question incorrectly," Professor Aisling offered meekly.

The Learnèd Custodian of the Answers merely looked down on him and waited.

"Medusa was cursed long ago and now turns to stone anyone who looks in her eyes, which is what Sebastian did. So how do we break Medusa's curse?" The professor looked around at his companions and nodded his head. Now they would get somewhere.

"'Medusa,'" read the Learnèd Custodian of the Answers. "'Greek beauty cursed with the power to turn to stone those who look in her eyes. See also: Perseus—'"

"No, we don't need Perseus," said the professor, becoming less patient. "What about curses?"

"'Curses,'" read the Learnèd Custodian of the Answers. "'Go boil your head; Go to Hades, or, variously, Go to Hades and stop at all seven levels; May you be struck with boils; May the fleas of a thousand camels infest your bed; May your barley crops fail unto the seventh generation—'"

"No, no, no!" cried the professor, unable to contain himself longer. "That's cursing *at*. We need curse *removal*."

The Learnèd Custodian of the Answers drew

himself up to his greatest height. He was the Learnèd Custodian of the Answers and did not allow trifling. In his haughtiest voice he said, "I have given you answers. Next querent."

Cassandra thought the Learnèd Custodian altogether too rude. Professor Aisling stood openmouthed, then turned for support to Captain Malachi, who raised his eyes to the ceiling and shrugged. The Oldest Professor, who had stood nearby during the exchange, nodded.

"I rather," *wheeze*, "expected," *huff*, "something like this."

The Learnèd Custodian had all the answers, which put him above the others.

The professor was unable to sleep that night. He arose in the wee hours and paced the corridor. From down a nearby hallway came the shuffling slap of slippers and the squeak of rusty wheels. Turning, the professor saw a bobbing candle flame, and soon the Oldest Professor shuffled near, pulling a stuffed owl on a low, wheeled platform.

"Professor Aisling," *huff*, "what brings you," *wheeze*, "out at this hour?"

"I couldn't sleep. I thought... I had such hopes for the Book of Answers."

"Yes, one does," *wheeze*. "One, quick," *huff*, "answer. So tidy," *wheeze*. "Lets you zip along," *huff*, "to the outcome without looking too closely," *wheeze*, "at the problem."

"What do you mean, sir?"

"Come along," *wheeze*. "I was just about to make," *huff*, "tea and toast." In a small sitting room, the Oldest Professor collapsed with a satisfied sigh into an overstuffed chair. He absentmindedly patted the owl on the head. Professor Aisling sat on an ottoman nearby.

"Now," huffed the Oldest Professor, pouring tea, "you mustn't think that the Book of Answers is without its uses. There are a great many questions that the Book is quite helpful with: What is the sum of eleventy-seven plus three; When did the Battle of Glettinflingle take place; Where does the sun rise; that sort of thing. But you haven't got that sort of question."

"I haven't? All I want to know is how to change a dwarf back from stone."

"Well," wheezed the Oldest Professor, "that's the short of it, but what about the long of it?"

"But what *is* the long of it?"

"Ah, there you are again, wanting to shorten the question. The long of it is the long of it."

"I don't understand."

The Oldest Professor pulled a thread from the raveled sleeve of his robe. "D'you see this thread?" Professor Aisling nodded dutifully. "Well, this is your question, 'How do we unstone our dwarf?' But as you can see, this thread is not the whole robe. The thread is the short of it, but the whole robe is the long of it."

"I wish I knew how to put all of this together," Professor Aisling muttered to himself.

"There are many other realms of study within the College. I should think one of them will help." The Oldest Professor then arose creakily and, taking up the string for his owl on wheels, went off to his chamber. With a sigh, Professor Aisling sought his own bed. When at last he fell asleep, he dreamed of his daughter Cassandra. She held out a bit of thread, and he heard her voice as if in echo: "Something bad will happen, bad will happen, will happen, happen...."

The long and the short of it.

When Cassandra awoke the next morning, her father sat near her bed, looking like his old self. Without thinking, she reached out to him; then, remembering all that had happened, she burst into tears. Her father held her while she sobbed. When her crying finally subsided, he leaned his face near her own and whispered, "Please forgive me, Cassandra. I wasn't listening, and all the time you were telling me the truth."

"I didn't mean it when I said I hated you," she whispered into his collar.

"I know," he whispered back.

After breakfast, the Oldest Professor proposed to take them round the College. They began at the College's east side, and no lab or lecture hall was passed up as unimportant. Miranda, though, went to the garden. Like the *Basset*, the College was much bigger inside than out, and it bothered her.

Research at the College of Magical Knowledge

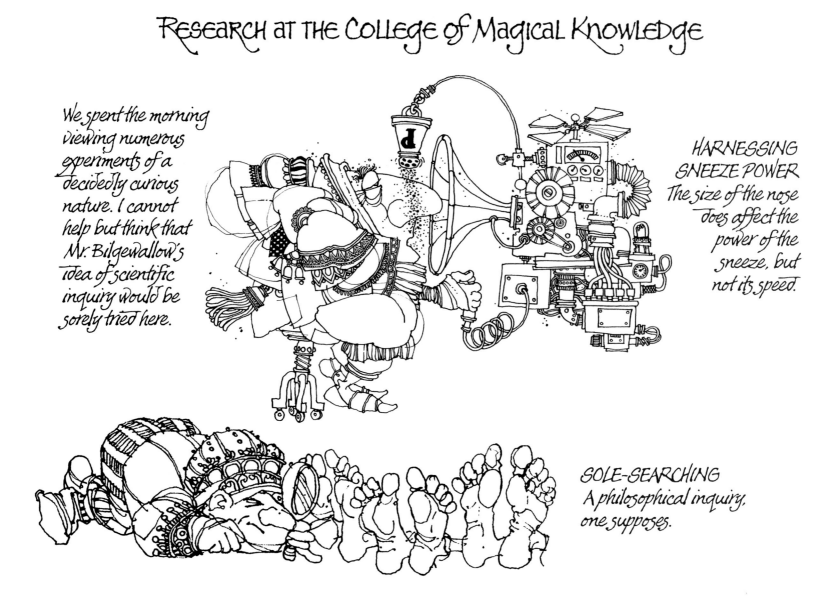

We spent the morning viewing numerous experiments of a decidedly curious nature. I cannot help but think that Mr. Bilgewallow's idea of scientific inquiry would be sorely tried here.

HARNESSING SNEEZE POWER
The size of the nose does affect the power of the sneeze, but not its speed.

SOLE-SEARCHING
A philosophical inquiry, one supposes.

Are the bird's
opinions part of
the query?

BIRD HUNTERS
WEARING CAMOUFLAGE
Apparently catching birds is less
important than proper use of
tools and equipment.

Is the whistling
part of the
camouflage, or
a way of passing
the time?

Decoy

SNAIL MAZES
The IQ of snails makes this
a slow process. Often
combined with a study
in contemplation.

[121]

In one of the rooms, they found a man standing on a long-suffering turtle's back while balancing an extraordinary number of diverse objects. "How does the clock balance atop the fish?" they wondered. At first, the man didn't notice them because he had to constantly shift his position to keep his collection aloft.

"Whoa-ho! Hey...uh oh!" he cried suddenly, leaning dangerously to the left to maintain his balance as he noticed he had company. "Hello... yikes!" and he contorted himself to keep everything aloft. Once more reasonably in control, he looked again at Cassandra. "But you're not a dwa...whup-uhp-uhp! Got it!" Cassandra, who didn't dare to speak, simply stared. As soon as one disaster had been averted, another waited at hand and needed to be dealt with.

He then noticed the others. "What? More of you? Hello...hey! Whoa!" He hastily changed his stance and just barely saved the cake perched precariously on a shoe. Some of the items seemed to be kept in the air by will alone. "So, what brings visitors to this...Whoops!..." He stretched and swayed wildly to recapture his treasures.

"You know, Malachi," Augustus said quietly to the other dwarf, "he's got at least six new things since I saw him last."

"...part of the College? Whoa! Uhp-uhp-uhp! Aha! Gotcha!"

"It seems," wheezed the Oldest Professor, "that while on an adventure our old friend Sebastian has been turned to stone."

"YI! No, no, can't balance him—Oop-oop-oop! He's too heavy. Ay! Uhp-uhp-uhp!"

"We're not trying to balance him," Professor Aisling said. "All we really need to know is how to change him back, and that's just the answer we can't seem to find."

"Well, you know—Whoa-ho-ho!—that could be where you're out of—Hey! Uhp-uhp-uhp!—balance. If you can't find—Yi-yi-yi! Uh-oh! Ah—an answer, maybe the problem is—Uh-oh! Oh! Aaaaa—within your question."

"A pity there's not a Book of Questions," said the professor a bit crossly.

"But there is," answered the Balancing Man.

"What? No one said anything about a Book of Questions!" said the professor.

"Well, actually," said the Oldest Professor, "you didn't ask."

The Balancing Act

The Keeper of the Questions was in an out-of-the-way part of the College, up a winding stair, down one long corridor, up eleven steps and beyond an oddly shaped door.

"What is it that you want?" the Keeper asked.

"We want our companion Sebastian, who has been turned to stone, returned to his old self," said Professor Aisling.

"Eh?" said the little fellow. "Turned to stone? How did that happen?"

"He looked into Medusa's eyes," answered the professor.

"And why did he look into Medusa's eyes?"

"So that my daughter Cassandra would not meet Medusa's lethal gaze."

"How did your daughter Cassandra come to risk looking into Medusa's eyes?"

"Because I had shouted."

"And why did you shout?"

"Because I was angry."

"Why were you angry?"

"Because Cassandra had told me that Captain Malachi was right."

"What was he right about?"

"That I had lost my faith in my great vision."

"What was your great vision?"

"That by believing, one sees."

"Why did you discard the vision?"

"I was excited and preoccupied by having found proof of what I believed."

"When you found that proof, you lost the vision?"

"I did…yes, I suppose I *did*!" answered Professor Aisling.

"Does this work?"

"No," said the professor, as his eyes lit up.

"Why not?"

"Because when the vision is gone, no amount of proof can replace it."

"What do you wish to do now?"

"I want to bring Sebastian back."

"What have you done to further this?"

"I have searched through every scientific text and treatise aboard the *Basset*."

"Why was this not successful?"

"Because mythology is not part of such books."

"Are there no texts on mythology?"

The Book of Questions is another way of finding an answer.

"Of course, but I know all the Greek myths. There are none that tell of bringing someone back from stone."

"What limited you to Greek mythology?"

The professor looked first shocked, then surprised. Cassandra watched him, knowing he was thinking very hard, searching through all his memories. Finally, the light of recognition glimmered in his face. He turned to Captain Malachi.

"I don't suppose any of you know where we might find a unicorn?"

While the professor and the rest of the *Basset* crew went in search of someone who might know where to find a unicorn, Eli girded up his patience and went back to the Learnèd Custodian of the Answers. He asked what ways one might use to prevent a curse from reaching its target.

"'Curse, prevention,'" read the Learnèd Custodian. "'Aardvark, skin only, worn as a cloak on

Eli smoked a pair
of spectacles over a
sooty candle flame...

Midsummer's Eve; Abacus, attached to a ram's horns; Aconite, leaves and flowers, made into a potion and painted on the doorstep; Adam's Apple, of deceased uncle preserved in red wine; Agate, polished, worn at the left temple; Agrimony, tied to one ankle; Allspice, in a cookie, crumbled and placed in a leathern sack and sewn in a coat lining; Antonym, shouted at dawn on St. Maurice Day; Apples, green and mashed, carried in a toad blad-

der; Artichoke, steamed with garlic and applied as a poultice to the soles of the feet; Artemisia, worn in the hatband; Axle, suspended from the northeast corner of one's domicile...'"

And that was just the A's. But Eli, who had brought parchment and a quill, dutifully wrote down every one of them, all the way through to "Zither, played by a maid of sixteen during a thunderstorm." There was nothing to indicate which curse could be prevented by which prevention, but Eli had heard something interesting way back in the G's: "Glass, smoked, worn over the eyes." That one showed real promise, he thought.

When he returned to his companions with his list, the professor greeted his discovery with delight. They straightaway had a pair of spectacles thoroughly smoked and put in a little satin-lined box to deliver to Medusa.

After consulting with several members of the College, the travelers learned that an ogre named Olaf from a small fishing village nearby was renowned as a woodsman. If anyone would be able to find a unicorn, they all agreed, it would be Olaf.

They rowed back to the *Basset*, ready to meet the ogre and carrying a pair of spectacles for Medusa. At Medusa's door, the professor and Eli had a polite dispute over who would take the first chance to see if the spectacles worked.

"I shall not participate in such nonsense," said Medusa through her door. "I shall want a crust of bread and a bit of time alone on the forward deck."

Medusa put on the spectacles and went above, where all was silent except for the birds that flew around the *Basset*. Holding the bread, she persuaded one little fellow to land on her wrist. She looked at the little bird. It looked back, pecked at the bread a few times and then flew away.

Delighted, she scattered the rest of the bread and

went below with the news. The other passengers were equally pleased, since it is always nice

not to have to worry about being turned into statuary. Only the professor seemed a bit subdued. He was as happy as anyone that Medusa could go where she would and not worry about harming the hapless. What struck him as odd was how much he longed to look into her eyes, and how quickly his heart beat when he thought of doing so.

Cassandra, of course, would have said that since this was such a long adventure, perhaps there should be people falling in love all over the place.

. . . and Medusa's lethal gaze was tamed. Even the snakes were well-behaved.

assandra watched the shore as the *Basset* approached the fishing village where Olaf lived. She was both excited and anxious. She very much wanted Sebastian back, yet twice since they sailed into the little bay she had felt Titania's stone go cold as ice. It was only for a moment, but it had happened.

The captain, too, was anxious. Although he'd seen neither hide nor hair of trolls, he didn't want to leave the *Basset* unguarded. The Manticore and the Gryphon, trading battle stories and comparing scars, offered to stay with the ship. The Sphinx, who was twirling her fingers in the Manticore's mane, scratched the back of his neck and said that she would also remain. The Manticore made a noise somewhere between a growl and a purr, unable to decide if he were pleased or not.

Miranda said that she wanted to go. Her father and Cassandra were both very surprised. "If this works," she told them, "I want to see it with my own two eyes." Miranda didn't tell them the other reason she wanted to go. Ever since she had been a little girl, she had loved to hear stories about unicorns. She couldn't pass up the opportunity to see one. Cassandra was so struck by Miranda's change of heart that she missed the conversation between her father and Medusa.

Medusa declined to go ashore with them, though at first she gave no reason. "I had hoped that you might accompany us," the professor said. "Will you not change your mind?" The professor looked so disappointed that she smiled, but it was a sad smile.

"With my new spectacles I am no longer a *lethal* monster, but I'm monstrous still, a monstrous curiosity, the snake-haired lady, to be stared at by idle eyes. I won't endure that. Here at least I *belong*. And should these be damaged," she pointed to her smoky spectacles, "I am lethal once more, a danger to bird and beast and the only live companions I've had in centuries."

The professor nodded. He longed to touch her cheek and tell her she was in no way monstrous, but seeing the straight back and proudly lifted chin, he thought she might interpret such a gesture as pity.

A calm bay, but was it a safe haven?

Ogres

Ogres are distant relatives of trolls, but larger and even less polite. Fortunately Olaf and his aunts are rogue ogres who prefer tea and cakes and parties to chasing people or stealing cattle.

Once ashore, they asked the first villagers they reached—a group of dwarf fishermen mending nets—where they might find Olaf the ogre. "In there, most like," said one, gesturing with a thumb to where the forest began.

"Or you could go and ask Miss Odalie and Miss Ophelia," offered another.

"Where would we find Miss Odalie and Miss Ophelia?" the professor asked.

"Tea shop, up the village," said another.

They found the tea shop easily enough, and inside were two "ladies" who could only have been Miss Odalie and Miss Ophelia. Cassandra did her very best not to stare, but they were quite amazing. Her father approached their table and bowed very low.

"Professor Algernon Aisling at your service," he said. "Do I have the honor of addressing the Misses Odalie and Ophelia?"

The ogresses smiled rather flirtatiously. "I am Odalie," said the nearest, offering her taloned hand to be kissed. The professor reluctantly obliged.

"And I am Ophelia," said her companion, who also offered her hand. As the professor planted a polite kiss thereon as well, Ophelia asked, "What brings you to our village, Professor?"

So Professor Aisling gave them the entire story, because elderly ladies, whether ogres or not, prefer the long version, to be chewed on and gossiped over later. "So we come seeking Olaf, whose woodsman's skills are well known, in hopes that he can lead us to a unicorn," he concluded. Miss Odalie and Miss Ophelia smiled and nodded proudly.

"A compelling tale, young man," said Odalie. "And you are quite in luck. Olaf is our nephew and today is his birthday. We are awaiting him to begin the celebration. We would be delighted if you would join us."

[131]

"We cannot attend a birthday party without a gift," the professor whispered to the group. "What do we have with us? Anything that would serve?"

Everyone began pulling this and that from their pockets, or, in the case of gremlins, from their hats. Soon they had an interesting, though not actually very promising, assemblage of whatnots. Finally, one of the gremlins pulled out an only slightly battered deck of cards.

"Just the thing!" the professor said. "Now then, Captain, if I might borrow your silk handkerchief." The professor wrapped the cards in the cloth. Miranda surrendered a ribbon from her hair to tie it up, and they were at last ready to wish Olaf many happy returns of the day.

Olaf, carrying his ax, returned to the village as twilight fell. He was greeted along the way by most of the villagers wishing him a happy birthday. The ogre woodsman was quietly gratified by all the fuss and bustle in his honor and never quite stopped smiling.

Sitting down among his friends and the visitors, Olaf began to open the heaps of gifts that surrounded him. When he came to the deck of cards, his delight was unmistakable. He held the deck up, then inspected each card individually and finally pulled out his two favorites (the four of clubs and nine of spades) to show to the rest of the group.

After the last gift had been opened, Miss Odalie and Miss Ophelia brought in an enormous feast. When all of them had eaten their fill, the professor approached Olaf to ask about finding a unicorn. Olaf nodded sagely and said that, yes, he had seen one deep in the forest and would gladly lead them there on the morrow.

Olaf's birthday party was a great success.

They walked deep into the woods in search of the Unicorn.

In the morning, they set off on a broad trail into the forest, carrying Sebastian once again lashed to a pole. Olaf told them stories about the forest creatures while they walked, saying that many of the bird-calls they heard were the birds telling each other about how absurd it looked to walk instead of fly.

"There's a lot of merriment in the branches to see so many of us walking," Olaf commented. "See how they fly close to us? Listen. You can hear them

laughing." Once Olaf had pointed it out to him, the professor realized he could hear their laughter.

"And the Unicorn? Do you speak with it?" asked Professor Aisling. Olaf shook his head.

"I see it now and again, but it is quiet and shy. And I have never seen it bestow its magic."

"What is the place you're taking us to?"

"Just a quiet pool fed by a brook with a water-fall. We'll be there in a short while."

When they arrived at the pool, Olaf counseled them to be very quiet in speech and gentle in their movements. "And, of course, your maiden should stand a little way apart to call it," Olaf added mat-

ter-of-factly. The professor turned and looked at Miranda. Miranda, in turn, looked surprised and rather taken aback.

"What?...me? But...I didn't know anything about this!" said Miranda. "I don't know how to call a unicorn!" Everyone was staring at her, which made her very uncomfortable. "What am I supposed to do?" she asked, wringing her hands.

"Just, well, just be still and quiet," answered her father. Miranda stood still, but her heart was beating wildly. They were all waiting for her to call the Unicorn and she didn't know how. She wanted to wail, "I can't! I can't do this all by myself."

As much as she wanted to see a unicorn, Miranda had not expected to be the one to call it.

Cassandra walked to her side and gently took her hand. "I think perhaps you should look in the box Queen Titania gave you," she whispered.

"Yes," Miranda whispered back. "Yes! Maybe there's a little whistle or a jewel or something." She put her hand in the pocket of her dress—and two of her fingers went through a hole in the bottom. She turned pale and hid her face in her hands.

"Miranda! What's wrong?" asked Cassandra.

"I've lost it! There's a hole in my pocket. The box isn't there, and I don't remember when I had it last. If I hadn't kept this old dress…" Miranda turned to her father with tears streaming down her face. "And now you're making me do *this*! I can't…I don't…" She fell to her knees and began to cry inconsolably.

There was a sudden commotion among the gremlins. Three of them were pummeling one of their companions, shouting something in their odd language. Finally the gremlin pulled his hat from his head and reached in a hand. Out came the little box. He walked toward Miranda with his hand extended, chattering the while. "What's he saying?" asked Miranda.

"He found it on the *Basset*'s deck several days ago.

With a lift of the intricate little clasp, Titania's gift was revealed.

He was just saving it in case someone ever wanted it again, he *says*," Cassandra translated.

With a trembling hand, Miranda took the little box and thanked the gremlin (who was doing his best to put on an innocent face). She opened the box and saw soft, white fabric. "Is it a hankie?" she wondered. She sat and pulled the white cloth… and pulled…and pulled…and pulled. There seemed to be no end to it, but finally out came the last bit of fabric and she found herself holding a lovely white dress set with pearls and gemstones. "It's lovely, magical, incredible," she murmured to herself; then added, "But why, oh why, couldn't they have put it in a normal-sized box?"

In a small thicket, Miranda donned the marvelous dress. It was as if it had been made for her. She walked back to join her companions, all of whom (except Sebastian) stared at the transformation. She had put away girlhood with her old dress and had become a maiden.

[137]

Unicorn

The Unicorn's magic, especially the power of its horn to heal, is legendary. Gentle and sweet-tempered, it is attracted to those who are pure of heart and body.

13th-century design

Early depictions of the Unicorn were diverse and very fanciful.

From an 11th-century drinking horn from Salerno

The professor was stunned and not at all certain he was ready for Miranda to look so like a woman. "Surely there are still years yet for her to grow up," he thought. Looking into her young face, he saw confusion…and fear.

"Miranda," he said quietly, "er, you don't have to…well, are you sure that you want to do this?" Miranda looked up at her father.

"What?" she asked, looking tiredly confused. "But, Daddy, I thought you wanted me to do this. I just…I just don't know how." Although he racked his memory for just what a maiden must do, he couldn't remember any tale that described exactly what the young woman did to call the Unicorn.

With a tiny smile, Cassandra led her sister to the pool. "Remember that painting of Mama that's on the mantelpiece at home? Look into the water, Miranda," she said.

Miranda knelt down. Staring back at her from the water was a young woman so like her mother that she at last understood Titania's words. There, looking back at her, was her mother, as close as Miranda's own heartbeat. Tears slid down Miranda's cheeks and rippled the still water.

Believing, she thought, is choosing to see something wonderful or beautiful or even magical. She wanted to tell her father that she finally understood. But everyone (except Sebastian) was looking into the forest.

Only then did she hear the rhythmic sound of hoofbeats. The Unicorn cantered right toward her. Miranda looked into its wise and gentle eyes and was filled with awe.

"Am *I* part of this magic?" she asked herself. The Unicorn knelt beside her and laid its head in her lap. "I *am* part of this magic," she thought, filled with the wonder of it. She laid her hand gently on its mane and stroked softly.

For a time there was silence, even from the wind and the birds above. Miranda continued to stroke the Unicorn's mane. And then, without a word spoken by anyone, the Unicorn rose and approached the pool. It leaned forward and, ever so slightly, touched the water with its horn. The water began to sparkle and dance with lights.

"Now!" cried the professor. "Get Sebastian into the pool!" The dwarves cut the lashings on the pole and carried Sebastian into the water. But the pool was both deeper and colder than they had expected. Archimedes, bearing most of Sebastian's weight, slipped and lost his grip. Augustus, thrown off bal-

*Miranda discovered that she was
indeed part of the magic . . .*

ance, let go, and Sebastian tumbled into the depths of the pool, sinking out of sight.

With a cry of dismay, Cassandra ran toward the pool. Suddenly, with a great whoosh of water and with sparkles, bubbles, great splashes and noise, Sebastian leapt up from the cold pool, shouting, "Yai-ai-ai! Get me out of here!" Joyously, they pulled him up the bank.

The welcome might have lasted hours, so glad were they to have their friend back, but at that moment, Miranda shrieked. Picking up her skirts, she ran toward the forest, screaming, "OH NO, OH NO, OH NO! *TROLLS!*"

. . . as Sebastian was restored to them.

At Miranda's scream of warning, the trolls, who had hidden themselves in the forest, leapt out with fierce war cries. Skotos, full of blazing rage, thundered a command to grab the Unicorn. The terrified beast struck out with its front hooves. Avoiding these, two trolls wrapped their arms around its neck while another troll wrapped the slashing hooves with rope.

Skotos turned to the professor with an evil smile.

"Well, well, Professor Thief, we've come on troll *business*. We want the skull you stole from our lodge-house, and we want it NOW!" he shouted.

"I don't have it—" the professor began.

"LIAR!" screamed Skotos.

"We've been on your pretty

The trolls leapt forward in full battle dress.

boat—not so pretty anymore—and it wasn't there!"

"But it went overboard!" cried the professor. "It's lost, gone. I can't get it back."

"Liar!" hissed Skotos. One of the gremlins, beginning to tug on the professor's coattail, babbled something and took off his hat. Hastily but not unkindly, the professor pushed him back to where the other gremlins stood.

"Not now," he said in a harried voice.

"It was ours and you stole it!" screeched Skotos, working himself into a rage. "GIVE IT BACK, LIAR! THIEF! STEALER OF TROLL TREASURES!"

"I swear I don't have it!" the professor protested. "It's at the bottom of the sea, and I can't get it back!"

Skotos' face grew dark and his eyes narrowed. "No?" he asked quietly. "Can't get it back, heh? Well, we'll just have to replace it with something. Now, just what should we replace it *with*, Professor Thief, collector of *specimens*?" Skotos' eyes glittered with delighted malice, and he shouted to the trolls, "Strangle the horn-beast."

One troll began to squeeze the Unicorn's delicate neck, making it squeal in fright and pain. Immediately Olaf lifted his club and lumbered forward to help. But Miranda, who could never afterward recall where such foolhardy bravery had come from, shot past him like a white spear.

"Stop it! Stop it!" she screamed and hit the troll's middle with her outstretched arms. Down went the troll in a flurry of knees and elbows. Miranda reached out to the Unicorn, but before she had gone three paces, another troll came up behind her and, with one arm, grabbed her around the waist. He lifted her clear of the ground while she kicked and struggled. With his other arm, he grabbed for the rope holding the Unicorn.

Skotos then drew an old sword from a battered scabbard and leapt toward the professor.

But Captain Malachi, the only one of the travelers wearing a blade, drew his cutlass and engaged Skotos, easily parrying the troll's first rude thrusts. Cassandra, unnoticed, ran toward Miranda, who still struggled with the troll who had grabbed her. The Minotaur, hearing Cassandra's shouts, lifted his club and ran to where Cassandra was pulling the arm of the troll holding her sister. At that moment, Miranda squirmed around and bit the troll's arm.

With a cry of pain the surprised troll loosened his grip, and Miranda sprang free. Olaf, seeing his moment, swung back his club just as the Minotaur surged forward. The great club dealt the unfortunate Minotaur a sharp blow on the head, and he

tumbled senseless to the ground. Olaf turned with a cry of dismay and saw the fallen Minotaur.

The troll who had been holding Miranda took advantage of Olaf's distraction. Raising his club, he brought it down with great force on the ogre's foot. Olaf boomed a cry of pain, but he was not undone until a pair of trolls threw their joint weight upon his back. Even then, Olaf didn't fall, but the sudden impact knocked his club from his hand, and it rolled away out of his reach.

Professor Aisling had been running to Miranda when Skotos drew his sword. Seeing Captain Malachi engage the furious troll, though, the professor had once more turned toward the girls, but he

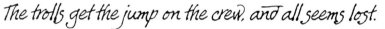

The trolls get the jump on the crew, and all seems lost.

heard Skotos give a guttural command to his lieutenant, Mog. In response, Mog raised a gnarled staff and slipped around behind Malachi.

As Mog rushed in to hit Malachi from behind, Professor Aisling raised his walking stick and dealt the troll a sharp crack on the wrist. Mog dropped his staff but immediately scrambled to reach it. The professor, using the walking stick like a javelin, gave Mog a hard blow to the ribs and knocked him, winded, to the ground.

Skotos, seeing his lieutenant down, drove Malachi backward with furious thrusts. With a wicked smile, he watched the Captain step back and trip over Mog, who was still rolling on the ground.

Laughing nastily, Skotos raised his sword over the fallen dwarf. Once again, the professor stepped forward and brought down his cane. The blow hit Skotos hard on the shoulders, giving Malachi time to roll out of the way.

The battle turned in the trolls' favor. Then, suddenly, help arrived from above.

Skotos turned and gave the professor an evil glare. Then he smiled again, a frightening gloat. With his sword he reached out and lightly, derisively, whacked the professor's walking stick.

"Not much of a weapon, Professor Thief," he sneered. "Perhaps I'll hang your head where little Gold-hair can see it when I take her home with me." With a bark of truly unpleasant laughter, Skotos raised high his sword.

A hawklike scream burst from the sky, and Skotos jumped back as the Gryphon swooped down bearing Medusa, who was suspended below. Jumping out of the improvised sling, she told the Gryphon to go back and bring the others. Skotos, seeing Medusa begin to lift her spectacles, swung the unfortunate

Mog between the Gorgon and himself. Then there was a terrific flash of lightning and a thunderous noise, and the trolls—even fierce Skotos, the Great Troll Leader—yelped like frightened dogs. Medusa found herself staring at a stone troll, but the wrong one. Fearing for her companions, she immediately slipped her spectacles back on just as Skotos shoved his stone companion over, knocking the professor to the ground.

"Keep your eyes closed!" Medusa shouted to the professor, giving him a moment to obey before once more lifting her spectacles.

But she never finished raising the lenses. In giving the professor time to respond, she had warned the troll leader of her intent. The professor shouted to her, but it was too late. Skotos slipped a leather bag over her head and pulled the drawstring tight behind her neck. She screamed and clawed and her snakes hissed, but Skotos tied a tangled knot and laughed. Once again he picked up his sword, but behind him the trolls began to yell.

Mog met Medusa, and the troll was truly petrified.

With an evil grin, Skotos closed in for the kill.

"The horn-beast! Catch it!"

The Unicorn, aided by the girls, had made it to the shadow of a rocky cliff. There, Miranda and Cassandra worked at untangling the rope from its hind legs. With a frustrated gesture, Skotos snarled.

"Everything," he said. "I have to do *everything*." And he raced toward the cliff.

Miranda and Cassandra knelt before the terrified Unicorn and struggled with the knotted rope. Miranda was wishing for nothing so much as a good pair of sharp sewing scissors, and so she was unaware of Skotos' approach. Cassandra looked up and screamed a warning, but Skotos leapt forward and grabbed her arm. He leered down at her, and then flung her toward Fracas.

"Hold on to the little Gold-hair. She's mine," Skotos barked. "Kill the rest."

He turned back to Miranda, still on her knees but trying as best she could to shield the Unicorn. Skotos' face grew dark with rage.

"You," he snarled. "I've had more than enough of *you*." Too many paces away, Professor Aisling disentangled himself from the stone troll and ran full tilt to save his daughter. But in his haste, he tripped over the ogre's club and fell sprawling. With a strangled cry, he scrambled to his feet, knowing with awful certainty that he was too far away, just as the troll chief began to raise his sword.

Skotos wanted to gloat over Miranda's terror, but she wasn't even looking at him, which made him growl and shriek. And still she stared beyond him. He would show her, he thought, and as he raised the sword high above his head, a huge shadow fell across him. He whirled toward it as a shout went up from his ranks.

THE DRAGON

Celestial Dragon, Kyoto, 16th century

Saint George and the dragon from Roger Van der Weyden c. 1432

A potent symbol in many cultures, the "winged worm" represented the connection between heaven and earth. In the Far East, dragons meant wisdom, wealth and good luck, while to early Europeans they were symbols of wickedness as well as strength.

"A FIRE DRAGON!" the trolls shrieked and ran for the forest. Skotos saw the great winged creature draw in a breath and knew there was only one way to save himself. He leapt, claws outstretched, toward Miranda and the Unicorn. If the Dragon wanted to burn him, he would have to roast the meddler and the horn-beast, too.

But Professor Aisling was there first. Heedless of Skotos' sword and the great breath of fire hot behind them, the professor pushed Miranda and the Unicorn away and covered both as best he could with his own body. In a blinding flash, a torch of intense flame lighted the cliff where Skotos had stood gnashing his teeth. Then it was silent but for the crackling and hissing of a small, hot blaze.

Professor Aisling arose and helped Miranda to her feet. Cassandra ran to her father and sister, clutching first one and then the other. The ogre limped to

where the Unicorn stood shivering. He knelt and removed the rope that held it, stroking it gently. Medusa finally succeeded in loosing the drawstring on the leather bag over her head. Coughing and choking, she ripped it off and threw it as far from herself as she could. Captain Malachi went to the Minotaur, who was woozily stirring, and helped him rise to his feet. Into this flew the Gryphon, the Sphinx and the Manticore.

"Where are they?" roared the Manticore, showing his teeth. Professor Aisling pointed to the forest.

"Well, let's go get them!" demanded the Manticore. "Finish them while we have the chance!"

From above them came a voice like the sound of a thousand rocks grinding together from far underground. In awe, the travelers as one looked up at the Dragon.

"No," he said. "Let them be."

f Cassandra hadn't been dusty and shaking and scared half to bits, she might have clapped her hands just to hear a dragon speak. She stared up at him. Of everything she had seen on the voyage so far, this was the most spectacular. He was huge and ancient and magnificent in a creaky, old-leatherish sort of way.

Miranda and Olaf were busy calming the Unicorn. Miranda smiled shyly at Olaf and asked if his foot still pained him. Olaf blushed and mumbled that it was quite all right, though the bruises had turned it rather blue. The Unicorn, free again, did not flee but pranced among the rocks, stopping at intervals to nuzzle Miranda's cheek.

Slowly, the travelers regrouped and brushed the dust from their clothing. Sebastian, who was near dizzy with confusion (and still wet besides), needed to have the cause of the melee explained. He was astounded at all that had transpired, for he remembered nothing since the moment he had leapt between Cassandra and Medusa. Hearing the tale, he inadvertantly glanced toward Medusa, who was (fortunately) wearing her spectacles, otherwise the whole affair might have started all over again.

Captain Malachi approached the professor with a concerned look on his face. "Professor, I'd as soon be making for the *Basset*. I don't know what kind of shape we'll find her in if trolls got at her."

"You needn't worry, Captain," said Medusa. "They must have sent a few of their number to the boat while the rest went hunting for the professor. I suspect they may have been more hungry than vengeful, for they made right for the galley, which was their undoing. No one enters the harpies' galley and makes a mess without consequences. The harpies had beat them back to the deck—and a sorry sight they were, too—when the rest of us

arrived. One glimpse of the Manticore's impressive teeth and they leapt overboard and scrambled onto a rather battered raft. I never even raised my spectacles." The Manticore's chest swelled proudly, and he made happy, rumbly growls. The Sphinx scratched the fur at his shoulder and whispered praise in his ear.

The professor's attention returned to the Dragon on the cliff high above them.

"Will you not come down?" called the professor. "We all owe you an enormous debt of thanks."

One of the gremlins ran up to the professor and tugged at his sleeve. He pointed to his hat and rattled off something. The professor looked at Cassandra. "He said it's in his hat," she replied.

"Righto," the professor nodded. "Amazing stuff in your hats. Now run along for a bit, there's a good chap."

Skotos had met his first and last live dragon.

With a groaning creak, the Dragon's leathery old wings spread above him. His bones complained like rocks in a spring thaw, and the skin rasped and whispered like aged parchment. But the ancient wings lifted him aloft, and he flew creakily down to where the travelers stood. He alighted in front of Professor Aisling, who spoke to him.

"I don't know by what fortune you found us here today, but we are most truly grateful for your help. For my own part, there are no words that could express my gratitude for your saving my daughter's life. I am deeply in your debt."

The professor drew his girls close to him and paused a moment before he spoke again. "Are you certain we should not dispatch the trolls now that they are scattered and disorganized, and their vile leader is fallen?"

"I am sure," he replied in a voice that sounded as if it grew out of the mountain's roots.

"Why?" asked the professor, for, after all, the trolls had threatened to kill Miranda and steal Cassandra. "From all that we have endured, we have seen that trolls are as unpleasant as they are untrustworthy. They tried to kill us—and would have succeeded but for you."

"Professor, they, too, belong to the land of stories. Legends once held an important place in the mortal world, but long ago most of mankind stopped hearing the greatness in the stories and heard only foolishness. Centuries passed, and with each turning of the world, mankind turned its face farther from us. Like most of my kind, I sought the peace of the mountain's root. Yet now and again, something calls me forth. Three times have I risen, and three times returned heavy of heart. And I awoke once more when I became aware of a mortal who went searching in peace for news of the old legends…I was amazed."

[154]

The Dragon's Tale

I shall set down here, as exactly as I can, the Dragon's own words, for they have changed forever my view of our history.

•

"The last of us sought the mountains during the time the Greeks called their Golden Age," the Dragon told me, "though we called them the Black Days. Already the stories of us had become less important, less part of the mortals' daily lives.

•

"And yet when I arose during early days of the Roman Empire, I saw that the Greeks had treated us well by comparison. Romans—except for the peasants amusing their children— told no tales of dragons. The heroes and gods had all taken human form.

"'Twas smoke that roused me next, when the great library at Alexandria was burned. As ancient scrolls fed the fire, men laughed, sure in the belief that their new knowledge was greater than ancient wisdom. Sorrow pierced my heart.

•

"There was a brief time when I thought great changes might occur. I arose and had many conversations with an enchanter called Merlin, who told me of the great king that was to come. Though I lingered in Camelot with hope, nought but brief glory and greater sorrow came to Arthur, and I swore never to return.

•

"But as I slept, I became aware of the actions of a mortal who believed, and I awoke once more."

The professor recorded the tale
of the Dragon.

"Not always in peace," the professor admitted ruefully, remembering the twice-stolen and now sunken dragon skull. "But always from this day forward," he added, squaring his shoulders.

"I had to see this mortal for myself," the Dragon continued as though speaking to himself. "And what did I see? Mortals risking their own lives for the mythological beings. I couldn't allow such folk to be destroyed." The Dragon sighed and looked at the professor. "But neither may we wantonly destroy all the trolls. Unpleasant they may be, and fierce and untrustworthy as well, but they belong here. They, too, are part of the legends."

Deep within the Dragon's eyes there arose an expression that on a human face would have been a slow, sad smile. He gave a deep sigh, as if recalling some vastly old and painful memory.

The gremlins had been still for about thirteen seconds. Then they babbled as incoherently as ever and began to use fallen tree branches as swords and javelins. The travelers were treated to a gremlin's-eye view of the trolls' attack. With a great deal of rushing about, the gremlins gave thrusts, parries and stumbles. As one of them dramatically portrayed the demise of Skotos, the captain said, "All right then, lads, enough."

Captain Malachi may have been told that the *Basset* was all right, but he was still ready to see his ship for himself. Although everyone was weary and drained from their brush with death, he urged them to hasten to the fishing village and they began the walk back.

Cassandra walked between the professor and Miranda, holding their hands. Medusa stepped to the other side of the professor and gently slipped her hand through his free arm. He turned and looked at her, once more wishing to see beyond the smoky lenses. She gave him a smile that made his heart begin to pound and utterly tied up his tongue.

They had not gone far when they heard the music of pipes gaily played and the sounds of singing and laughter. With a delighted gasp of recognition, Cassandra raced ahead through the royal procession of faeries, passing pipers and ignoring singers, and ran straight into Titania's welcoming arms.

"You'll never *guess* what happened, Queen Titania. There were *trolls* and they were going to *kill* us and then the *Dragon* came and burned the troll chief who was *horrible* and I saw it and…and there was a *unicorn* because Sebastian had been turned to *stone* and…" Cassandra stopped, shook her head and held her arms out wide as if to say that everything, just *everything,* had happened.

She burrowed farther into the queen's arms, feeling totally safe at last. All around, Cassandra heard the merry welcome of the faeries and their glad, triumphant music. There was exuberant explanation from all sides, but for a few moments, the little girl stayed safe in Titania's embrace.

Having recovered, the gremlins reenacted the great battle.

Small faeries helped the gremlins brush away dust and find their lost hats.

Miranda approached the entourage. Seeing the older girl, Titania smiled and held out her hand. Miranda took it, wondering why it had taken such an extraordinary adventure to understand how warm and kind Titania was.

"You were right, Your Majesty," Miranda said shyly. "My mother wasn't far away. I looked into the pool and I saw myself *and* I saw her." Miranda dropped her voice as though sharing a confidence. "And I was part of the magic. The Unicorn came to me, and I did know when to open the box. And the dress was so beautiful."

Miranda looked down at the gown, crestfallen. One sleeve was badly torn, and the whole garment was covered with stains and rips. "I'm terribly sorry about the dress. It really was so lovely."

"Well, let us see. Hmm. It doesn't look so bad." The queen, with quick little movements, brushed her hands over the dirty, torn fabric. "Yes," she said, drawing back and looking at Miranda, "it's not so bad at all."

Cassandra's eyes and mouth were round O's of absolute astonishment.

"Miranda, look!" she said, but her sister was already looking down at the dress. It was once more perfect, unstained and untorn, as wonderful as the moment when Miranda had first put it on. Miranda looked at the queen wonderingly.

"The magic goes on and on," she whispered.

"And that is as it should be," said the queen.

The king walked first to the Dragon with evident joy. He held out his hands in greeting.

"Old friend," he said warmly. "I did not dare to hope—and yet I had hope."

"The world has had little time or place for the old race," the Dragon said sadly.

"And yet you came," King Oberon added.

The Dragon slowly nodded his head. "I found mortals defending with their lives the creatures of legend," he said.

"And now?" asked Oberon. "What will you do? "Will you remain with us?"

"The story is not ended, but it is greatly changed from the ancient days."

"And dragons still belong in it," said Oberon. The old Dragon closed his eyes for some moments, remembering the eons past, the times that would never come again. "So be it," he thought, and he reopened his eyes on the new world.

"Yes," answered the Dragon at last. "Dragons are part of the story."

As Titania lightly brushed the torn fabric, the dress became whole and beautiful once more.

When Professor Aisling came face to face with Oberon, he didn't know what to say. He had not, as he had promised the king, kept his extraordinary vision. Though he had regained it, he wasn't sure what his reception would be. But Oberon walked directly to him with a warm smile.

"You are a most fortunate and well-chosen mortal, Professor Aisling," said the king.

"Well-chosen?" asked the professor.

"Yes, because of your belief," Oberon answered. "You cared enough about the myths to bring them together out of isolation. I cannot command the legends; I could but send my thoughts outward and give word of your coming."

"So that's how everyone seemed to expect our arrival!" the professor exclaimed.

"And you have succeeded beyond my fondest hope," Oberon continued. At such praise, the professor dropped his eyes. He was embarrassed, for

The professor realized that the dragon skull was not the evidence he really needed.

the king obviously had not heard the entire story about the stolen dragon skull.

"Ah, yes," said Oberon, as though Professor Aisling had spoken aloud. "Where is the evidence to show your skeptical colleagues?" Shamefaced, the professor prepared to tell the whole story. "It's—"

But one of the gremlins ran up to him and, tugging on the professor's sleeve, removed his hat. "Excuse me, Your Majesty," said the professor. He leaned down to the gremlin and said, "I know you fellows keep some extraordinary stuff in those hats, but I really—" Babbling, the gremlin sat down on the ground, placed his feet against the brim and began to pull something out of the hat.

The professor recognized it almost immediately (although another of the gremlins had to come up and pull on the crown to help get the mysterious thing out). The hat released its treasure all at once, and both gremlins went tumbling backward, one holding a hat, the other clutching the dragon skull.

"Ah, yes," said the king again. "Here we are: the proof." Oberon took the skull from the gremlin and held it out to the professor. "Something to take back with you to verify your journey, Professor."

Professor Aisling stood for a moment, embarrassed. Then, taking a deep breath, he stood up straight, stepped forward and took the skull.

He turned and walked to where the Dragon stood, and with a deep, formal bow the professor laid the ancient skull at the Dragon's feet.

"This belongs to your kindred, and I have no right to it," he said simply.

"But what about your disbelieving colleagues,

With a great deal of huffing, puffing and pulling, out came the huge skull.

Professor? What will you offer them as evidence?" asked Oberon quizzically.

"Nothing."

"Nothing?"

"Yes, Your Majesty. I cannot give anyone the magic and beauty of the legends by showing them this ancient skull, however magnificent. It was never *proof* that I needed, though I thought so for a time. The myths, and the way one delights in them, create the magic. The evening I first saw the *Basset*, all I had was my delight and wonder. I had my belief. That was the magic."

"Yes," the king added with a smile, "faith precedes the miracle."

"So, Your Majesty, proof is of no consequence. I do, however, have the answer I sought, to give to my old colleagues."

"An answer, Professor? To which question?"

"The one I had been asked by these selfsame colleagues: what good are a lot of old myths? And I shall answer: they are a window on the world, just as science is. The wisdom of stories and legends is that they give us another way to understand ourselves and the place we inhabit."

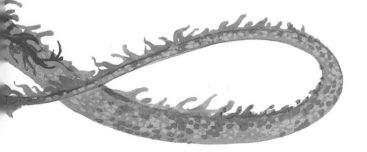

Carefully, deliberately, Aisling removed the smoked spectacles and gazed into Medusa's eyes.

Olaf promised to plant the dryad's tree.

The Gryphon offered to try all the harpies' new recipes.

"And what of these folk? Will they travel with you back to London?"

The professor shook his head. "No, Your Majesty. I cannot make them curiosities; they're my friends." He shook his head, having no idea what to do. "Perhaps we should sail them back to—"

He never finished. The Sphinx and the Manticore cried, "No!" simultaneously, and the Gryphon squawked. "Back to that wretched garden?" Medusa asked. "Indeed, I shall not go. I don't wish to be alone anymore." The others quickly agreed.

"But what are we to do?" asked the professor.

Miranda quietly and shyly stepped into the circle. "Excuse me," she said, "but that little mermaid island seemed to be a nice place. It was awfully pretty, and no one else lived there."

"A marvelous idea," said Oberon.

The king and queen, as well as all their followers, walked along with the travelers as far as the fishing village. The professor turned once more to Medusa and offered his arm. They strolled, lagging behind and talking. Leaving this lovely, surprising woman with the snaky locks was a heartache. He longed to tell her so, but the words tangled in his mind and he couldn't sort them out. If only he could look into her eyes, he thought, he might know how to frame the words his heart longed to speak. Suddenly remembering something King Oberon had said, he knew what he must do.

"All this time I've been traveling under the banner 'By believing, one sees,'" he said with a smile, "but when I look at you today, knowing that I must leave, I suddenly know exactly what it means."

"Professor—" Medusa began, hoping to forestall him. He reached toward her spectacles, and she quickly held her hands in front of them.

"Algernon! No!" she cried. "I couldn't *bear*—" But Algernon took her hands in his own, gently pulling them away from her face.

"Faith precedes the miracle," he said calmly, never taking his eyes from her face. He took away the smoky spectacles and gazed into her eyes. Several heartbeats passed in which Medusa dared not breathe. In the distance, they heard the others calling for them to hurry along. With a smile both warm and sad, the professor again offered Medusa his arm. She slipped her spectacles on, and they walked back to the others.

Miranda smiled through tears as she stroked the Unicorn's mane a final time.

Saying good-bye to Sebastian was the hardest thing Cassandra had had to do on the journey, even harder than seeing him turned to stone.

The Manticore and the Sphinx had one another for company. The Minotaur mooed sadly at Cassandra but looked forward to playing cards with Olaf.

FOND FAREWELLS

They took their leave of the faerie folk as the tide turned. Miranda carefully put away the white faerie gown, but not for her old, everyday dress. She poked around the *Basset* and found several pretty dresses. These, everyone agreed, made her look quite a lady. Cassandra began to think that perhaps it wasn't so awful to grow up.

They sailed into the bank of fog and dropped anchor. Soon they began to hear the sweet, mysterious singing of distant mermaids, and before long the unseen sea serpent began to spirit them toward the mermaid island.

There, Cassandra renewed her acquaintance with the sea serpent, the mermaids and the shy, colorful coral faeries. Miranda, who was getting used to being a lady, wouldn't go into the water. She did, however, explore secret flowery places, and wherever she went, the Unicorn was nearby.

On the morning of their departure, it suddenly occurred to Cassandra that she must leave Sebastian and go home. She burst into tears. Seeing this, Sebastian tried to be gruff, but soon had to get out his handkerchief and snuffle quietly into it. They walked together and sat on a rock by the water, and Sebastian told her of the dwarf families who live on the Plunwijitt Isles and only see each other every seven years during High Feast Time. "They keep each other near in between by telling stories about each other," Sebastian told her.

But at last all preparation was completed. The dwarves quietly began to ready the *Basset* for the final leg of the voyage. While they all made their smiling, tearful good-byes, the professor offered his arm once more to Medusa and, saying nothing, they walked along the beach.

When the tide turned, the *Basset*'s sails were unfurled, and the little ship sailed out of the bay. Medusa stood on the beach, listening to the rhythmic swish of waves over sand. As the afternoon sun turned the ship's mast and sails to gold, a single tear rolled from beneath one smoky lens and journeyed down her cheek.

EPILOGUE

here you have it, Gentle Reader. The Aislings sailed back to the land of mortals. But, as you may know, a magical adventure, once begun, is never quite over. In later decades, the Aislings prospered. Cassandra found that growing up wasn't so very terrible. She missed Sebastian and the Minotaur a great deal, but discovered that if she wrote down everything she remembered about the voyage, it kept her friends close to her heart. Cassandra's father was greatly changed by the voyage. He returned to the university with enthusiasm and happiness. But it was a more profound change than even Cassandra knew.

The professor didn't allow the many changes in the world to cast aside the study of the old myths. Smartly slapping his walking stick on the desk of a Bilgewallow or Sneedsnippet, he could give six and eighty excellent reasons why the myths were important, not the least of which was that imagination, not the slide rule, was the mother of progress.

Miranda fulfilled the promise of her beauty and much more. She chose to marry a kind but disorganized young cleric. On her wedding day, she wore a lovely white dress that confounded ladies far and wide who demanded to know what the fabric was. She merely smiled and said that she thought it might have been made of moonbeams and moth wings, which no one sensible believed. Miranda bore six children and, with her help, her husband's parish became quite orderly, very organized and exceedingly well kept.

Cassandra delighted, as her father did, in the old myths. She kept to her studies and also spent time transcribing her father's notes. In her twenty-fourth year, she and her father made a journey to Greece. After an evening's lecture, a young botanist followed them (which fondly reminded Cassandra of the Minotaur) back to their inn. He apologized for his boldness but, having heard Cassandra speak, he was impressed by her intelligence. He asked if he might call on her.

Cassandra said that he might. She later told her father that she would probably have to keep the botanist, since he'd followed her home. They were married shortly thereafter, and Cassandra, too, wore the white dress. The same ladies asked again about the fabric. "I haven't an idea," Cassandra told them. "It was a gift from the Faerie Queen," which none of them believed either.

The professor never remarried but was happy for many years with his work. When he began to think about retirement, he told his daughters and they both offered places in their homes, to which he replied, "Perhaps."

So, imagine the daughters' surprise when they went to visit their father one afternoon and found neither hide nor hair of him. At last they went to his study, where they noticed something odd. Small portraits of each of them in the faerie gown were gone, as was his most recent journal. Most surprising of all, on his desk lay a pair of smoked spectacles.

Miranda raised her eyebrows and said, "You don't think…" In answer, Cassandra reached up to clasp the necklace Titania had given her. Holding the stone, she could just make out the swish of waves, the shuffle of a battered deck of cards, merry voices welcoming a returning friend—and the whispery hiss of snakes. With a smile, Cassandra told her sister what she heard. Miranda thought once more how surprising and mysterious life was, and quite lovely besides.

"The magic just goes on and on," she said.

And that, Gentle Reader, is as it should be.

—THE END